**Saman[...]
what he was up to**

"I still don't understand why you want to pretend our separation is over."

"You don't have to understand," Craig replied. "Just follow my lead," he added softly before his lips claimed hers in a slow tantalizing kiss. Involuntarily Samantha's lips parted, inviting him to explore her warm sweetness.

But instead of continuing the kiss, he moved away from her. "That's all we have time for now," he drawled softly. "We'll try again later."

"Don't count on it," Samantha retorted, pretending a coolness she wasn't feeling. "You promised you wouldn't force me to do anything."

"And I'll keep that promise," he replied with a soft ironic laugh. "But I get the impression that kissing me is something you want to do."

Books by Flora Kidd

HARLEQUIN PRESENTS

HARLEQUIN ROMANCES

These books may be available at your local bookseller.

For a free catalog listing all titles currently available,
send your name and address to:

Harlequin Reader Service
P.O. Box 52040, Phoenix, AZ 85072-2040
Canadian address: Stratford, Ontario N5A 6W2

FLORA KIDD

passionate pursuit

Harlequin Books

TORONTO • NEW YORK • LONDON
AMSTERDAM • PARIS • SYDNEY • HAMBURG
STOCKHOLM • ATHENS • TOKYO • MILAN

Harlequin Presents first edition April 1984
ISBN 0-373-10682-3

Original hardcover edition published in 1984
by Mills & Boon Limited

Printed in U.S.A.

CHAPTER ONE

SAMANTHA CLIFTON parked the cream Cadillac belonging to her father-in-law, Howard Clifton, in the parking lot of Antigua airport, got out, locked the doors and walked towards the entrance to the terminal building. Bright sunlight blazed down, shooting sparks off chromium car fittings. Palm trees swayed in the hot trade wind. Luggage porters, package tour guides, taxi drivers and tourists swarmed together in front of the entrance, a colourful noisy crowd of people. The Air Canada flight from Toronto had just landed, bringing a load of Canadians escaping for a week or two from the bitter February weather of their homeland to laze about on the beaches of this particular island in the sun.

There was a certain reluctance in the way Samantha approached the crowd of people and began to push her way through towards the open doorways of the building. She hadn't wanted to come to meet the person she had been asked to meet. In fact she had dallied as long as she could in St John's, the capital of the island, where she had spent the morning shopping and then having lunch, and it had even occurred to her not to come to the airport but to drive to another part of the island, to spend the afternoon at one of the beautiful resorts, perhaps at Halcyon Cove, and pretend she had forgotten to go to the airport.

Not seeing the person she had been asked to

meet, she stepped through one of the doorways into the arrivals area of the building and looked around. There were still a few tourists inside looking hot and alien, overdressed for the climate, struggling with their luggage, but she couldn't see Craig anywhere.

Perhaps he hadn't come after all. Perhaps some urgent business had prevented him from leaving his offices in the Clifton Building in Toronto. Samantha moved forward slowly, still looking around, half hoping she wouldn't see him and yet half hoping she would see him too, at the same time chiding herself for being so mixed up in her emotions. But then Craig had always had this effect on her. Theirs was a strange love–hate relationship.

'Looking for me?' drawled a masculine voice behind her.

Samantha stiffened against the shiver which chilled her spine and she turned slowly to look at the man standing behind her. Eyes as grey as slate, and about as hard, set beneath impatiently slanting dark eyebrows in a taut tanned face looked down at her, and she felt the old antipathy towards this man, Craig Clifton, her husband, rise up within her; an antipathy which was immediately overwhelmed and drowned by a surge of pleasure on seeing him again, a dangerous disturbing feeling; a purely sensual reaction to his presence. 'You're late,' he added coldly, giving no indication that he was pleased ... or not ... to see her.

'The flight arrived earlier than scheduled,' she retorted, shaking her head back as if to shake away the feeling of pleasure, her reddish brown hair, casually cut to fall in rough waves, swirling on her smooth sun-kissed shoulders left bare by the simple sundress of purple-dyed Sea-Island cotton she was wearing. From under her darkened eyelashes she gave him a cool sea-green glance. 'Do you have much luggage?' she asked. 'Should I bring the car over to the kerb?'

'No, this is all I have. I can carry it to the car,' he replied. He had one suitcase and a zipped holdall, slung over one of his shoulders.

Samantha led the way across the road to the parking lot, dodging between taxis and mini-buses. While Craig heaved his case and holdall into the back seat of the car she slid behind the steering wheel and started the engine. Taking off his suit jacket—it was made from sleek grey alpaca—and also his tie, he tossed both of them on top of his case and then sat down beside her.

They drove away from the airport along a winding road past untidy fields. When they reached the junction with the main road which links St John's with the southern tip of the island Samantha turned the car to the left, away from the capital city.

They had gone several miles and had crossed the flat spread of tawny-green land of a big cattle ranch before either of them spoke. Then they both spoke together as if neither of them could stand the tension which was twanging between them.

'How long have you been at Cliff House?' he asked.

'Why haven't you come before?' she queried.

He laughed softly, a pleasant yet mocking sound, and half turned in his seat to look at her. She gave him a quick sidelong glance and felt again that dangerous stirring of her senses. She'd hoped she would feel nothing on meeting him again after two years of separation. She'd thought she'd got over being in love with him.

'We're still doing it,' he murmured, and shifted nearer to her putting his left arm along the back of her seat behind her shoulders.

'Doing what?' she asked, straightening her back and sitting up primly, away from contact with his arm.

'Thinking along the same lines and then speaking together even though we haven't been together for some time.' Craig paused, then added quietly, 'It's good to see you, Samantha.'

She didn't reply because they were approaching a village, a cluster of wooden houses with shady verandahs over their front doors. Brilliant flowering vines climbed over walls and fences and small gardens seemed to burst with coconut and banana palms. The main street was narrow and twisting and she had to slow down to avoid some merry-faced, brown-skinned school children who ran out into the road in front of the car, daring her to run them down, playing their game of 'chicken' and laughing at her tauntingly when she slowed the car almost to a stop before they darted away and let her go on.

'I've been here nearly a week,' she replied, answering his question.

'Really?' He sounded surprised. 'Why did you come?'

Samantha flicked a puzzled glance at him. Was his surprise for real?

'I came because Carla wrote to me saying that Howard had been very ill and wanted to see me.'

'Did she tell you she'd written to me too and

had passed on the same message?' he asked. His fingers drifted lightly upwards over her bare shoulders to the nape of her neck and stroked it suggestively, playing in her thick hair. Gritting her teeth, Samantha willed herself not to react to that provocative caress and kept her gaze on the road before her.

'I didn't know until this morning when Carla asked me to meet you at the airport,' she replied coolly. 'She told me then that she'd asked you to come on Howard's behalf, but you'd replied saying that you couldn't come until you'd finished some business negotiations.' She gave him another sidelong glance. 'Just like you to put business before anything else; before your own father's feelings.' Her voice grated scornfully.

Her remark had the effect she had wanted it to have. He stopped playing with her hair and moved away from her. But she knew he was still looking at her. She could *feel* the stare of those wintry grey eyes; observant eyes that didn't miss any detail of her face, her hair, her clothes; shrewd eyes accustomed to weighing up opposition or competition.

'So what about you?' he retorted. 'How come you were willing to leave that all-demanding job of yours to fly out here and visit your father-in-law? I hadn't realised you were so fond of Howard. What did you hope to gain by yielding to his demands? A mention in his will?' Sarcasm gave his voice a harsh edge.

I mustn't let him make me angry, Samantha warned herself, gripping the steering wheel so hard the knuckles of her fingers showed white through the sun-tanned skin. *I always lose when I let him make me angry.*

'I'm fond of Howard,' she replied quietly. 'And of Carla. Both of them have always been very kind to me.' Suddenly emotion broke through her control. 'I came because ... because he's very ill, because he's dying. Don't you know that? He's dying!'

'Yes, I know that.' Craig spoke tonelessly.

'So I couldn't refuse to come,' she went on. 'I couldn't refuse to yield to the wishes of a dying man even if you could.'

Silence again while they drove through the village of Liberta, passing the church of St Barnabas. Built over a hundred years ago of Antiguan green stone and known locally as the Chapel of Ease, the quaint little church was a tourist attraction and stood at a sharp bend in the main street of the village. Samantha guided the big car cautiously round the bend and out of the village. The road before them twisted past green hills thick with vegetation, many different kinds of palms mingling with tall evergreens like the cola nut tree and the eucalyptus, as well as flowering trees such a poinciana and low-growing shrubs of many different kinds.

'And what about your job?' asked Craig casually, ignoring her jibe.

She darted another uneasy glance in his direction. He was leaning back against the car door, a dangerous position, his broad shoulders blocking out the light, his eyes narrowed to slits as he stared at her.

'I gave in my notice ... a few weeks ago,' she admitted, looking back at the road.

'So you're out of work?'

'For the time being, yes,' she replied, hoping he

wouldn't ask her why she had left the women's magazine where she had been working in the editorial department, not wanting him to find out she had lied to him when she had said she had given in her notice. The truth was she had been asked to resign when the publishers of the magazine had decided to cut back the staff in an economy drive. Her job had been considered redundant.

Silence again. The sun beat down on the car and she was glad of the air-conditioning. The road was dipping down now towards the village of Falmouth and beyond the straggle of houses Falmouth Bay glinted blue and gold in the afternoon sunlight. On the left the schoolhouse, grey and bare, loomed up. Samantha slowed the car down, flicked on the indicator and turned on to a narrower country road which twisted uphill. The surface of the road was pitted with potholes, making driving along it a slow and tortuous business. Cream-coloured goats grazing on the grass at the sides looked up to stare at the passing vehicle.

'Why have you never touched the money I've sent to your bank account?' asked Craig in that sudden direct way of his.

'Because I haven't wanted it,' she replied. 'Because I prefer to be independent of you.' Her voice rose a little shrilly in spite of her resolve to speak to him coolly and reasonably. 'Why have you continued to send me money?'

'Because you're still my wife.'

'You ... you could have divorced me,' she said, her lips quivering even though she was doing her best to keep them stiff. 'Why haven't you?'

'Why should I?' he retorted. 'You've given me no reason to divorce you.'

'I . . . I left you, deserted you. Isn't that reason enough?' she said in a low voice, gripping the steering wheel hard again and keeping her gaze fixed on the winding rough road but hardly seeing it.

'Not to my way of thinking. I think I understood at the time why you left. You wanted out for a while, to come to terms with yourself, find out what it is you want from life, so separation seemed like a good idea. But I've always hoped that we'd get together again some day. When you'd grown up. When you'd stopped behaving like a spoiled child,' Craig said coolly.

A red haze seemed to shimmer before Samantha's eyes. He was always so calm and arrogant; always pretending to be so righteous while making her appear to be in the wrong.

'I'm not a spoiled child!' she retorted furiously, turning her head to give him a glinting green glare.

'Hey, watch out!' he warned. 'You're going too fast! Slow down, or we'll hit that . . .'

He seized the steering wheel and swung it violently to the right, and the big car swerved dangerously off the road.

'Take your foot off the pedal,' Craig rasped as the car lurched precariously on the soft shoulder of the road. 'I said take it off, not put it down, you fool!' he roared.

What he was saying penetrated through to Samantha at last and she became aware that the car was plunging forwards down a slope through undergrowth and over rocks, the branches from bushes scraping along the paintwork.

'Brake, brake!' Craig shouted, and she put her foot down hard on the brake pedal. The car's tyres slid on dry grass and it came to a shuddering and abrupt stop a few inches away from the twisted trunk of a tree as the engine stalled.

'Oh, why did you do that?' she flared. 'Why did you pull on the steering wheel?'

'Because you were going like a bat out of hell for one of the biggest potholes I've ever seen, and you could have destroyed the car, to say nothing of damaging yourself and me,' he retorted. 'You weren't looking where you were going. I had to do something. You still have one hell of a temper, Sam.'

'Well, it was all your fault. You made me angry, calling me a spoilt child the way you did. You always make me angry. That's why I left you.'

Reaction to what had happened set in and she began to shake. Covering her face, with her hands she cried out,

'Oh, why did you have to come here? I wish you hadn't come! If I'd known you were coming sooner I'd have arranged to leave before you came. I wish Carla had told me you were coming yesterday and then I could have moved out. I wish she hadn't asked me to meet you. Oh, oh, it's going to be awful with you here! Oh, I can't bear it—I can't bear to be near you. I'll have to go away!'

Words poured out of her, babbling incoherently, but eventually stopped as she grew short of breath. The silence which followed her outburst was hot, somnolent, broken only by the chirping of small yellow birds that flitted among the scrubby trees. Samantha kept her face covered and her shoulders heaved with the violence of her emotions, but her ears were very alert as she waited for Craig to move or to say something to her.

After a while he did move, but not towards her. He opened the door beside him and got out of the car. Piqued because he hadn't tried to reason with her or make some reply to her tirade, Samantha lifted her face from her hands and looked around. Hands in the pockets of his well-cut grey pants, his head tipped forward, he was examining the position of the car. He didn't seem to be at all put out by what she had said to him. He was more interested in the car than he was in her. Well, that figured, she thought stormily. The car had cost more than she had.

'We're going to need help to get out of this fix,' he said calmly, raising his head to look at her. 'Sounds as if there's a vehicle coming down the hill. Go and stop it, please. Whoever is driving it can help to push us out of here.'

'Go and stop it yourself,' she retorted sulkily.

'Oh, come on, Sam, you know the driver is much more likely to stop for you than for a tough-looking guy like me.'

'Suppose the driver is a woman?' she challenged, tilting her chin at him.

'Then she'll stop for another woman who seems to be in distress, of course,' he replied, his lips tilting up at the corners in a grin that robbed his lean face of its usual hardness. 'Won't she?' he added, his eyebrows tilting in mockery. He came towards the car and opened the door beside her. 'Come on, get out and go up to the road before the car passes us, please,' he said, offering her a hand to help her out.

'Oh, all right,' she muttered ungraciously, but she didn't put her hand in his. She was determined to avoid all physical contact with him. She dared not risk touching him or having him touch her, she realised. She had been too long without him, too long without making love to him and with him to be close to him now and behave rationally.

Sliding past him, she climbed up the slope to the road, reaching it just in time as a car came round the bend and down the hill. Waving her arms, she ran out into the roadway. The car, a big blue Pontiac with a taxi sign on its roof, squealed to a stop. The driver looked out at her, his brown face glistening in the sunlight, his dark brown eyes round with surprise.

'Please, can you help us?' said Samantha, waving an arm towards the other side of the road. 'We had to drive off the road to avoid a pothole back there and now the car is stuck. Do you think you could help us push it back on to the road?'

'We'll be pleased to do that, miss,' he replied with a wide white grin. 'Won't we?' he added, turning to look at the other men who were in the car, all of them youngish, all of them big and strong, presumably all of them workers from the government-owned hotel nearby, on their way home after a days' work. 'Just show us where the car is,' said the driver.

Within a few minutes the Cadillac was back on the road and the taxi was departing downhill in a cloud of dust.

'I'll drive the rest of the way,' said Craig, who was already in the driver's seat, having guided the car up the slope while the other men had pushed it. Samantha didn't argue because she didn't really enjoy driving along that particular road. It was too full of obstacles. She sat down in the passenger's seat, closed the door and they were off again.

They didn't talk any more. Craig concentrated on driving, on avoiding more potholes and vehicles coming the other way, and Samantha looked out at the scenery, at the tawny-green land sloping down and then rising up to distant hills. At the deep blue sky across which big puffs of afternoon cumulus sailed like over-canvassed galleons. The road took a sharp curve to the left and there was the sea, an even deeper blue than the sky, dappled with silvery light, changing colour near the coast from near-purple through pale azure to green where yellow sand shone upwards in the shallows.

On a long peninsula of land the roofs and walls of the government-owned hotel glinted among clustering palm trees. On one side of the peninsula was a bay, protected from the wind. On the other side was a lagoon formed by a long reef of coral over which waves crashed continuously, sending up showers of white foam.

The end of the road which led down to the hotel was reached and passed. The Cadillac purred onwards steadily past some small wooden houses where washing fluttered from lines, brown-skinned children played ball games.

Only a few miles to go now to Cliff House. Howard Clifton had built the residence on the forty acres of land he had purchased over thirty years ago when, with an exclusive circle of wealthy people, all of them from either Canada or the United States, he had discovered the beautiful island of Antigua lying like a fallen lopsided leaf in the brilliant blue waters of the Caribbean Sea, and had started a trend towards millionaire hideaways in the tropics.

Howard was still a multi-millionaire, but because of poor health he had come to live permanently with his second wife Carla in the sprawling ranch-style bungalow built on a cliff overlooking a quiet remote bay. Although, as chairman, he still took a close interest in the world-wide operations of the business he had developed, he now left the day-to-day supervision to Craig, his eldest son, the only child of his first marriage to Ashley Colter, daughter of an impoverished English aristocrat, whom he had met when he had first visited Antigua. Ashley had been granted a divorce from him years ago after a long and particularly bitter suit.

Samantha glanced at Craig. He didn't look much different. Eight years older than she was, he was now thirty-three, but the angle of his jawline was still taut and his straight wiry hair was still jet black and his figure was still lean. His skin too was just the same, looking tanned even though he had only just arrived from Canada. According to his mother, the beautiful and delightfully haphazard Ashley, who had been at the wedding, the tawny tint of his skin was due to the possibility of there being Red Indian blood in the Clifton family.

'The first Clifton to go to Canada was an explorer and adventurer and is supposed to have set up house with the daughter of an Indian chieftain, an Iroquois, apparently. That's why their skin is that reddish-brown colour. It's possibly the reason why they're so silent and deep.' Ashley had laughed. 'Actually Howard is too silent and too deep for me,' she had confided. 'I never did find out what makes him tick, apart from the making of millions.' Ashley had become more serious and her grey eyes had considered her daughter-in-law's fine-boned pink and white face. 'I hope you'll be luckier with Craig than I was with Howard, my dear. Remember he has something of me in him, that he isn't hard all the way through. He likes to live and laugh. He likes to love, too. Remember that.'

It hadn't been hard to believe what Ashley had said about Craig during the first few weeks of their marriage, thought Samantha now, while they had been on their honeymoon, sailing about in the yacht belonging to his father, cruising among the islands of the Bahamas. Craig had been full of love and laughter at that time; he had been gentle and courteous, teaching her many things; how to sail the boat, how to dive for conch and how to make love.

She was conscious suddenly of a strange stabbing pain, low down, and she caught her breath sharply. She hadn't wanted to remember their honeymoon. It always gave her a pain to recall those wonderful halcyon days of sunshine, blue skies and blue water that they had spent together among the pretty green and yellow desert islands, when she had been so much in love with the man who was sitting beside her; when she had been caught and trapped in a spell of romance.

It was nearly four years since she had first met him in London. She had been just twenty-one and very pleased with herself, excited by her job with a publishing company that had published not only a national daily newspaper but also several magazines, including one which had been aimed exclusively at women. She had worked in the publicity department of the women's magazine, writing up copy for advertisements. She had been a sort of apprentice, learning all she could about the production of a magazine; learning about layout, content, business management and circulation, her ambition to be, one day, editor-in-chief.

Young and enthusiastic, brimful of the feminist idealogy drummed into her by her strong-willed politically-minded mother, she had also been somewhat naïve, completely unknowledgeable then about the machinations of big business; about take-overs by powerful companies of smaller companies. She had certainly never heard of Clifton Enterprises Inc., an Canadian company that owned a newspaper chain in Canada, another in Australia, and was looking for ways of owning a British newspaper publishing business.

So it hadn't been surprising that when she had been asked to show a young man called Craig Clifton around the offices where the women's magazine was produced she had had no idea that he was the heir apparent to a multi-million-dollar business. She had liked him on sight, she remembered now. She'd liked his directness, the way he had treated her as an equal, asking her intelligent questions about the magazine and listening to her answers—at least, he had looked as if he had been listening to her while she had been speaking to him, staring at her intently with those slate-grey eyes.

But after she had shown him around the offices she had never expected to see him again, and she had been sincerely surprised when he had come back the next day to the publicity department and had invited her to go to the theatre with him that evening. She had accepted the invitation gladly, for the tickets had been for the musical *Evita* which she had longed to see but for which she had been unable to get tickets.

During the next few weeks they had met many times, having found that they had many interests in common and had enjoyed each other's company, yet not once had Craig told her of his relationship to Howard Clifton, the multi-millionaire newspaper owner, or why he was in England. All he had ever told her about himself was that he was from Canada, that he worked and lived in Toronto and that he was in England to represent his company.

Then he had disappeared from her life as abruptly as he had appeared in it, without telling her he would be going away and without telling her he would be back too. Samantha had been hurt and had been surprised at herself because she had always considered herself to be very liberated in her attitude to the opposite sex and most unlikely to fall in love with a man after having known him for such a short time.

It had been the worst spring of her life as she had struggled to forget him and had failed. Her days and nights had been haunted by memories of the way he looked, the way he talked and the way he had kissed her. Then one Friday evening in June, just as she had been leaving the offices on the building on the South Bank of the Thames where she had worked, he had walked in as if he had never been away. Ignoring the two other people who had been with her, he had kissed her on the mouth and had said in his cool direct way,

'Will you marry me, Samantha?'

And she had been so pleased to see him that she had flung her arms about him and had said,

'Oh, yes, I will. Yes, please!'

Samantha became aware that the car was slowing down. Shaking away memories, she looked through the windshield. The road was sloping down a hill and she could see the water of the small sheltered bay, rimmed with yellow sand and guarded by two rocky headlands. The road took a sharp twist to the left to curve round to the head of the bay and came to an abrupt stop where there had been a landslide at one time, preventing the continuation of the building of the road because beyond the jumble of rocks the land fell away sheer to a small sandy beach, fringed with sea-grapes and palms.

The car turned through an open gateway on the left and swept up a smooth driveway edged by two rows of stately royal palms. The driveway ended in a courtyard of red tiles before the arches of the entrance to a long low building. Rough cream-washed walls glowed in the sunlight. Over the wide picture windows there were blue and green awnings. The roof was geranium red.

The car had hardly stopped when a man came down the shallow steps. He was Jeremiah Smith, Howard Clifton's butler, and his closely cropped hair clung to his brown skull like a black woollen cap. His short white jacket, white shirt and white trousers were immaculate. His brown face was serious yet calm, his black eyes sad.

'Welcome, Mr Craig,' he said with the typical good manners and soft voice of the Antiguan native. He opened the door for Samantha to get out of the car and then turned to the back of the vehicle. 'I'll take your case in, sir. I expect you'll be wanting to shower and change. I'll show you to your room.'

'Thanks, Jeremiah. How have you been?' asked Craig, showing as he always did that warm interest and consideration for anyone who worked for the Clifton family.

'Can't complain, sir. Can't complain,' replied Jeremiah sedately, lifting out the suitcase and then slinging the holdall over one shoulder. He glanced at Samantha as he closed the car door. 'Mr Farley was asking where you were, Mrs Samantha. He said was to tell you he'll be waiting for you at the poolside,' he added, his brown face expressionless.

'Farley?' Craig exclaimed, swinging round to look at her, his eyebrows slanting in a frown. 'How long has he been here?'

'He was here when I arrived last week,' she replied.

'But he's supposed to be at Harvard. This half-year semester isn't through yet.'

'I . . . think . . . he hasn't been well and Carla decided he should come here for a holiday,' Samantha replied hesitantly.

Craig looked very annoyed. He muttered some imprecation and turning on his heel marched up the steps, his suit jacket slung over one shoulder. He disappeared into the dim hallway.

Samantha waited for a few moments before she followed him. The cool entrance hall had a tiled floor, was furnished with simple wooden couches covered with lime green cushions, and it went right through this central part of the bungalow to a wide sliding glass door which opened on to the wide concrete apron of the swimming pool.

The pool was sheltered on two of its sides by the other wings of the bungalow which were set at right angles to the main building. On the fourth side it was screened by trellises over which flowering vines grew in profusion. Samantha strolled around the pool to one of the striped umbrellas and sat down at the table beneath it, knowing she was screened from any of the windows overlooking the pool by an arrangement of potted orange trees and other decorative plants.

The young man was was swimming in the pool saw her and swam to the side and climbed out. He was thin and not very tall. He was so thin his ribcage showed clearly through his darkly tanned skin. His hair was black and curly and so long its wet tips brushed his shoulders. His eyes, like those of his Latin-American mother, Carla Clifton, were big and dark. He flopped down on one of the chairs at the table.

'Has he come?' he asked.

'Yes.'

'Did you tell him I'm here?'

'No, Jeremiah did that when he gave me your message. Craig asked me why you're here.'

'And?'

'I just told him that you'd been ill and Carla had made you come here for a holiday.'

'What did he say?'

Samantha's soft pink lips twitched into a faint smile and she shrugged her gold-tinted shoulders.

'I'm not sure, but it sounded rude,' she replied.

'He's angry, then,' muttered Farley lifelessly. Suddenly he put his elbows on the table and clutched his bowed head with both hands. 'God, what am I going to do?' he muttered. 'He'll give me hell when he knows I've dropped out of Harvard.'

'I didn't know you'd dropped out,' exclaimed Samantha.

'Neither did I until this morning, when I decided that I can't go back there. It doesn't matter what my father or what Craig says, I can't go back. I'm not made of rock.' Farley let out a dreary little laugh and gave her a rueful glance. 'He's well named, isn't he? Craig means rock, doesn't it?' He paused, then went on in a shaky voice, 'I can't go back. I'll have another nervous breakdown if I go back. I just couldn't take it any more. He lowered a hand and covered hers which was resting on the table. 'Thank God you're here, Samantha,' he went on softly. 'You understand about facing Craig and telling him how I feel, don't you? You know what it's like to dash yourself against his rock-like will.'

'Yes, I suppose I do,' she murmured.

'Then you'll say something to him on my behalf?' he pleaded, leaning towards her hopefully. 'You'll try and make him see how unfitted I am to making a career in business? You'll tell him that what I want more than anything is to be a performer, to entertain people with my songs, like my mother used to do?'

'I'll try.'

'Thank you, thank you,' he whispered, his Latin temperament showing as he raised her hand to his lips and kissed it. 'I love you, Samantha, do you know that?' he added, a red light seeming to glow in the depths of his dark eyes. 'I love you, and I wish you weren't married to that unfeeling rock-like monster, my half-brother. I wish we could go away somewhere together, you and I . . .'

'Farley, stop it! Please behave,' she urged, trying to tug her hand from his grasp.

The leaves of one of the potted orange trees rustled as someone pushed past them. A shadow slanted across the table, and Samantha looked up. Craig, naked except for the bikini style swimming briefs he was wearing, stood framed by the plants. He was looking down at her and Farley's clasped hands.

CHAPTER TWO

'DAMN!' Dropping her hand as if it was a hot coal, Farley sprang to his feet and faced Craig, a flush of dark red suffusing his cheeks. 'Look, it isn't what you're thinking,' he spluttered anxiously. 'I . . . I was just thanking Samantha for . . . well, for being here and for being . . . for being helpful, that's all.'

'I see.' Craig's eyebrows went up in mocking surprise, but he wasn't really amused, Samantha could tell, because his voice had frostbite in it and the glance he gave her froze her with its icy hostility. He looked back at Farley. 'I'm surprised to find you here. Since when has a university term finished in the middle of February?'

'Excuse me,' Samantha murmured, rising to her feet. She had no wish to be a witness to a quarrel between the two half-brothers. 'I have things to do, and I'm sure you two have a lot to talk about.'

'But, Samantha, you promised!' wailed Farley.

Ignoring his plea for help, she turned away from the table and was going to step past Craig on her way to the house, but he sidestepped in front of her and she found herself looking at his chest, at the warm, tanned skin lightly beaded with sweat stretching across muscle and bone, at the dark crisp hairs arrowing down to his navel. Her hands curled into fists at her sides as she struggled to control an upsurging impulse to touch him intimately.

'Not so fast,' he said quietly. 'It's you I want to

talk to, not Farley. Come swimming with me—not here, in the bay. We can sunbathe afterwards on the beach.'

'No, I can't. I ... have things to do,' she whispered, suppressing a longing to do as he asked; to go with him down the steps cut in the cliffside to the tiny crescent-shaped beach, to swim and play with him in the silken salt water and then to lie with him, close to him, possibly in his arms on the warm yellow sand under the shade of the sea-grape trees. 'No,' she whispered again, and pushing past him hurried away from him into the wind-cooled dimness of the hallway.

High heels clicked on the tiled floor and Carla appeared from the passageway which led to the east wing of the bungalow where Howard Clifton had his suite of rooms. Her full-bosomed shapely figure was swathed in a simple dress of black and white printed cotton, her coarse and curly black hair was piled up on top of her head and her heavy-featured, fleshy face was thickly rouged and powdered. The make-up, although skilfully applied, couldn't hide the lines which anxiety had carved into her cheeks, nor could it cover up the anxious expression in her black eyes.

'Howard heard the car returning,' she said. 'Has Craig come? Did you meet him at the airport? Is he in the house?' Her accent was slight, merely a distortion of some vowels, and her voice was soft and deep. Samantha always thought of molasses when Carla spoke, thick, dark brown and liquid. Carla was from Venezuela. She was a kind, generous but very tempermental person, sincerely religious and totally devoted to Howard and to their son Farley.

'Yes, Craig is here,' Samantha replied. 'He's out by the pool with Farley.'

'Ah, no!' Carla looked extremely worried and she seemed to surge across the hallway towards the wide open doorway leading out to the poolside. 'What is he saying to Farley?'

'I don't know. I didn't want to hear,' said Samantha curtly.

'But I would have thought he would have gone straight to see Howard,' exclaimed Carla, swinging round to face her. 'Ah, doesn't he have any feelings, that one? Is his heart made of stone?'

'I don't know,' said Samantha. 'Carla, I wish you'd told me before this morning that he was arriving today.'

'But how could I? I didn't know until this morning when his secretary phoned from Toronto to tell me he had just left to catch the plane coming here.' Her dark eyes narrowed and she stepped closer to Samantha to peer curiously at her. 'What would you have done if you'd known before this morning?' she demanded rather excitedly. 'What would you have done?'

'I'd have left Antigua, gone somewhere else— anywhere,' replied Samantha wildly. 'I don't want to be here while he's here. I can't stay in this house while he's here. I'll have to go away . . .'

'Ah, no, no, no, you mustn't leave. You must stay here. You must, Samantha!' Carla was actually wringing her plump beringed hands. 'You mustn't go. Howard wants you here.'

'I wish I knew why. I wish I knew why he invited me to come.'

'He has not told you?' demanded Carla, looking surprised.

'No. He talks very little when I go to see him. All I do when I'm with him is read to him.'

'That is why you must stay,' said Carla emphatically. 'You can do something for him that I can't do. You can read his favourite books to him, Dickens and Hemingway and the others,' she gestured grandly as if she was heaping all the great novels of the world together. 'I do not read English well and I do not understand English and American literature. But you do. He says you read beautifully and it gives him great pleasure to hear you reading. Ah, Samantha, you cannot leave now, not while Howard is enjoying your company. And it was his idea that you should come and stay for a while. He knew, you see, that Craig would come if you were here. And he was right, wasn't he? Craig has come as soon as he heard from me that you were staying with us, he dropped everything and flew out here.' Carla's eyes flashed with triumph.

'You mean. . . .' began Samantha, breaking off when she heard the sound of Farley's voice, shrill with anger.

'Ah, *dios mio!*' exclaimed Carla distractedly, the wrinkles deepening as she frowned. 'I must go. I must go and stop them.'

She whirled out through the doorway on to the pool's apron, and Samantha walked down the passage which led to the west wing of the bungalow where a small suite of rooms had been allocated to her. The small sitting room, furnished as the rest of the bungalow was in sea-colours ranging from purple to palest aquamarine and furnished with simply designed teak furniture, was just as she had left it that morning. She walked

across it and into the bedroom, pulling up short by
the doorway when she saw the grey jacket, grey
pants and white shirt that had been flung down on
the purple bedcover of the wide king-sized bed. On
the floor Craig's handsome leather suitcase lay
open, clothes foaming untidily out of it. The
zipped holdall was on a nearby chair.

Craig had come and had arrogantly assumed he
was going to share this bedroom with her. He had
come and had invaded her privacy, scattering his
clothing across her room, making his presence felt.
Yet she was sure Carla had arranged with
Jeremiah to put Craig in a bedroom near his
father's, on the other side of the house, far away
from her.

Voices raised in anger drew her attention to the
sliding patio window which was open and
overlooked the pool. She went over and looked
out. Carla, Farley and Craig were standing
together not far away. Both Carla and Farley were
talking at once, actually shouting at Craig, both of
them gesticulating wildly. Still as a statue carved
from one of the western red cedars which grow in
Canada, his skin glowing in the sunlight, his arms
folded across his face, Craig was listening to them.
Or was he? His head was tipped forward and he
seemed to be staring down into the pool.

Suddenly he raised his head and looked round,
right at the window where she stood, as if he had
sensed her presence. Samantha stepped back
quickly and ran across the bedroom, through the
sitting room and into the passage. She ran right
along the passage to the hallway and out through
the front door, down the steps. Past the gleaming
Cadillac she ran, slowing down to a walk only

when she was on a path twisting through a shrubbery of exotic flowering shrubs, on her way to the rough steps cut into the cliffside.

At the bottom of the steps the small beach was deserted save for a pelican which took off with a great flapping of its big wings. Sunlight and shadow dappled the yellow sand and the pale green water lisped at the edge of the shore. Under the shelter of wind-bent sun-bleached trunks of sea-grape trees and palms, on a wooden rack which had been built especially to hold them, there were two windsurfers, almost flat white fibreglass boards with their masts and sails.

Taking off her sun-dress to reveal that she was wearing a sleek black and blue striped *maillot*, an all-in-one, strapless swimsuit which clung closely to her trim figure, Samantha lifted one of the boards and its mast and sail from the rack and carried everything down to the water's edge. She stepped the mast in the slot in the surfboard, then pushed the board out into the water, wading out with it until it was floating freely. Holding the mast upright, she climbed on to the board until she was sure which way the wind was blowing, then sidling around from the front of the mast to the side of the board she pulled in on the fishbone boom which held the sail. The sail filled with wind and the board leapt forward, tipping over under the weight of the big yellow and red sail. Shifting her weight, and bending her knees, Samantha pulled hard on the boom, counteracting the strength of the wind, and the board surged forward even faster.

Like a one-winged butterfly the little craft skimmed over the shallow waters of the bay.

Water chickled crisply under the board and wind hummed in the sail. Right across the bay Samantha sailed, totally absorbed in what she was doing because if she lost her concentration and failed to see any shifts in the wind she was likely to capsize. She sailed until she reached a small semi-circle of yellow sand gleaming between pinkish grey rocks beneath the overhanging cliffs of one of the headlands.

As soon as she was in the shallows near the shore she let go of the sail. The mast tipped sideways and the sail swooshed into the water. Wading, she pushed the windsurfer ashore, took the mast out of its slot and pulled it up on to the rocks, spreading the sail out to dry. Then she lay down on the sand to let the sun dry her, knowing she would be undisturbed because the small beach was inaccessible from land. Only in a dinghy or on a surfboard could it be reached.

It was good to be alone for a while, to feel the sun warming and drying her skin, and she was glad she had found this place not far away from Cliff House which she could reach without having to ask if she could borrow a car or if she could be driven to it. Farley didn't like windsurfing, so he had never accompanied her on her daily expeditions to this hidden beach since she had come to the island.

Lying on her stomach, she pillowed her head on her arms and closed her eyes. She wouldn't be able to lie in the sun for long, just for a few minutes to increase the tan on her arms, legs and shoulders. How quiet it was! Only the lapping sound of the water against the store, the rustle of the wind among the leaves of sea-grapes, the occasional cry of a seagull.

But her mind wasn't quiet. It was full of turmoil, roaring with confusion because Craig had come. Was it true what Carla had said? Had Howard only invited her to come and stay at Cliff House because he had guessed Craig would come once he knew she was there?

She frowned and opened her eyes. Taking a handful of sand, she let it trickle through her fingers. Surely if Craig had wanted to see her during the past two years there had been nothing to stop him from calling to see her in London. He had known where she had been living and working. But he had never come to see her since they had decided to separate, and he had never asked her to return to live with him in Toronto either.

Would she have agreed to return if he had asked her? Would she have agreed to a reconciliation if he had made the first move? Deep down she knew very well that she would, that she had been longing for him to turn up suddenly and tell her he loved her and couldn't live without her. Sometimes, when she had felt in low spirits, she had been tempted to resign from her job and fly out to Canada and tell him she had had enough of being separated and that she wanted more than anything else in the world to live with him again, to be a part of his life again. Only pride and the memory of Morgana had prevented her from giving into the wild yet natural impulse.

Morgana. With a groan Samantha closed her eyes again and immediately she had an image of Morgana floated across her mind's eye. Morgana Taylor. Tinsel-like ragged curls framing a thin triangular face; huge dark tragic-looking eyes; a

small pursed mouth painted a vivid red. Morgana
Taylor, daughter of another rags-to-riches Canadian millionaire, who had made a name for herself
as the author of several witty novels about the
feminist cause. Morgana Taylor, whom Craig had
been going to marry once.

Morgana had appeared suddenly, like a raised
ghost, at the Clifton table at a charity dinner held
to raise money for a writers' centre in Toronto.
Her white skin and white-blonde curls set off by
the clinging black gown she had been wearing,
which had been held up by two thin straps over
her shoulders, she had greeted Craig in a soft
fluttery voice, her dark eyes sending what
Samantha had sardonically called 'bedroom
messages' to him. Rising to his feet politely, Craig
had presented Morgana to Samantha.

'Your wife?' Morgana had explained. 'But,
darling, I had no idea you were married! When?
Where?'

'Nearly a year ago in London, England,' Craig
had smiled at Samantha. 'Did you realise we'll
soon be celebrating our first anniversary?' he had
whispered to her.

Room had been made at the table for Morgana
to sit next to Craig, and from then on she had
monopolised his attention, talking to him in a
fast low monotone, completely ignoring Samantha,
Bill and Judy Felton and the other well-known
writers Clifton's Enterprises had invited to dine.

'Who is she?' Samantha had asked Judy when
they had both gone to the women's rest room
together.

'She's the woman Craig was going to marry
before he went to London and met you,' Judy had

replied as she had leaned forward to look at herself in the mirror while she applied lipstick.

'They were engaged to be married?' Samantha had exclaimed.

'Not exactly engaged. Morgana doesn't hold with old-fashioned conventions like engagements. But it was assumed they would marry. They've known one another for years and both Conrad Taylor, Morgana's father, who's president and chairman of a big investment company, and Howard Clifton, looked kindly on the match. It would have been the amalgamation of two big business fortunes.'

'What went wrong?'

'No one knows.' Judy had glanced at Samantha's reflection in the mirror and remarked dryly, 'Why don't you ask Craig?'

Samantha had asked him, that night when they had been preparing to go to bed in the elegant master bedroom of the house where they had lived on the outskirts of Toronto.

'Judy told me that you and Morgana Taylor were going to be married at one time,' she had said abruptly as she had turned down the covers on the bed and had slid between the sheets.

'Did she?' he had answered noncommittally, pulling on his pyjama pants.

'Were you?' she had persisted, bothered by new and rather ugly feelings. She had been married to him nearly a year and had just realised she had known nothing about his life before he had met and married her. She had been too much in love, too fascinated by the physical aspect of their marriage to have given much thought to other women he might have known before he had met her. For the first time, that night, she had known what it was to be jealous. The feeling had been violent and shocking.

'Was I what?' Craig had replied tantalisingly, sliding into bed beside her.

'Were you once going to marry Morgana Taylor?'

He had flicked off the bedside lamp and darkness had swirled about them. Shifting closer to her, he had put an arm about her waist and had slid a leg suggestively across both of hers. His fingers had played in the lace trimming of the low-cut bodice of her nightgown. As he had leaned over her her nostrils had filled with the warm scents of his hair and skin, and desire had zigzagged through her.

'I've never wanted to marry anyone but you,' he had whispered, then his lips had covered hers and that was the end of that particular conversation.

But it hadn't been the end of Morgana. She had kept popping up; at parties at the homes of Craig's friends; at dinners to which he and Samantha had been invited; at the yacht club; at the golf club—and everywhere she would monopolise Craig's attention, greeting him always with a fond embrace, a kiss and a hug, excusing herself smilingly to Samantha by saying that her affection for Craig was purely sisterly.

'We grew up together,' she would say. 'Our back yards were adjoined.'

Perhaps if she had had more to do, if time hadn't lain so heavily on her hands during that first eighteen months of her marriage, Samantha wouldn't have been so jealous of Morgana. Perhaps if she'd had a job . . .

She had made the suggestion that she should get a job to Craig, had even asked him to help her find one in the publishing business, and had caused their first serious quarrel. He had been adamant in his refusal to let her go to work, and when she had argued with him he had retaliated by becoming very silent and withdrawn. He had turned off.

Perhaps if she had become pregnant, had had something to look forward to, she wouldn't have been so susceptible to jealousy of whatever Craig did when he wasn't with her. And he had been away often, travelling to different countries on business. Perhaps if she had been older and more experienced, more knowledgeable about people, perhaps if she hadn't been a stranger in a strange land without the support of close friends and relatives, suspicion wouldn't have eroded her love and trust.

But then Craig was also to blame for what had happened. He had helped to contribute to her suspicions and her jealousy by his refusal to talk about his personal life before he had met her. He had been so secretive, so silent.

Then one day she had heard that on one of his business trips he had been seen with Morgana, that he and the author had actually been staying in the same hotel.

Hurt and bewildered, Samantha had accused him of having arranged to meet Morgana on that particular trip. He had denied that he had.

'Then she must have known where you were going and she went there deliberately, to be near you, to be with you,' she had accused furiously.

'Now why would she want to do that?'

'Because . . . she . . . she thinks you belong to her . . . still.'

'I belong to her?' he had repeated, and had laughed. 'Oh no. I don't belong to anyone except myself,' he had added softly. 'And you'd better believe it. Any more of these displays of possessive jealousy on your part and we part company, you and I.'

'Oh, I see,' she had seethed, her redhead's temper getting beyond her control, aroused as usual by his calm coolness. 'So I'm supposed to sit back and say nothing while you and Morgana carry on an affair, am I? Right under my nose, too! Well, you're quite mistaken about me. I refuse to be cheated in that way. I'm leaving. I ... I'm going home!'

'Home? Isn't this your home?' he had demanded.

'No, it isn't. I don't feel at home here, in this house or in this country. I hate it!' she had burst out childishly. 'I want to go back, to England. I want to go home!'

'Then of course you must go home,' he had agreed quietly, and she had been surprised and more than a little hurt because he had been able to let her go so easily.

It had been wonderful at first to be back in England, to bask in the affection of her family, and it hadn't taken her long to confide in her mother about her suspicions concerning Craig's relationship with Morgana Taylor.

'Well, I'm not really surprised,' Brenda had said. They had been walking in Epping Forest at the time, enjoying the touch of spring in the air on a surprisingly warm February day.

'Why aren't you?' Samantha had asked.

'I tried to warn you when you told me he'd

asked you to marry him. I felt you were blind to the reality of the situation,' Brenda had replied in her serious, didactic way. Trained in educational psychology, she was fond of analysing behaviour. 'He comes from such a different background. And then he's been used to having a lot of money all his life. He's had everything he could ever want, so his attitude to women tends to be on the chauvinistic side. You shouldn't have married him. You should have waited a while before making any commitment to him. If you'd waited you'd have probably decided that being married to a wealthy businessman with a playboy mentality wasn't what you want. If you'd waited you'd have found out what you know now about him and this other woman without having to go through the marriage ceremony and you'd have been free to change your mind about him. Do you want to stay married to him?'

'I . . . I don't know,' Samantha had muttered. 'I haven't asked myself that question yet. Oh, I'm all mixed up! I was so happy, at first. I loved him and I liked being with him. I still love him and like being with him. But I don't like it when he goes away and leaves me on my own. I don't know what to do with myself.'

'You could go to work,' Brenda had suggested. 'Couldn't you get a job in publishing in Toronto?'

'Craig won't let me.'

'Won't let you? How can he stop you?'

'He doesn't want his wife to go to work, he says, and if I try to get a job he'll interfere and prevent me from being hired. He suggested I joined some women's groups and did volunteer work, so I did. But somehow, for some reason, I didn't fit in.'

'I can't believe that a daughter of mine would allow a man to dominate her like that!' Brenda had exclaimed. 'Can't you see you've made a mistake in marrying him?'

'But I love him,' Samantha had wailed.

'Stop talking rot!' Brenda had snorted. 'Romantic love is a myth, and the sooner you realise it the better. Craig Clifton rushed you into marriage before you had time to think probably because he couldn't get you into bed with him unless he promised to marry you first. You always were a bit straitlaced about pre-marital sex.'

'That isn't true,' Samantha had retorted. 'Craig never asked me to sleep with him before we were married.'

'Then why did someone like him, the heir to millions, choose to marry you?'

'I . . . I used to think it was because he liked me for myself,' Samantha had whispered unhappily.

'But now you're not so sure.'

'No, I'm not so sure. Oh, Mum, I don't know what to do!'

'Stay here a while longer,' Brenda had advised. 'Let him make the next move.'

It had been easy to agree to stay, and she had been in England for over a month before Craig made any move. Then he had arrived one day, and she had been so overjoyed to see him that for a few days and nights everything had been blissful and she had forgotten her doubts and suspicions. Not until he had asked her to return to Canada with him did they have one cross word.

'I'd really prefer to live here near London,' she had replied cautiously.

'Why?'

'I've been offered a job,' she had ventured.

'Where?' he had demanded, frowning at her.

'On the editorial staff of *Woman's Insight*.'

'That's a Clifton Enterprises publication now.'

'I know that. I remember that's why you were here eighteen months ago. You came to help negotiate the take-over.'

'I can always put pressure on, make them withdraw the offer to you,' he had said sharply.

'If you do ... I'll ... I'll leave you,' she had retorted breathlessly. 'Oh, can't you see, Craig, I ... I'm not suited to be your wife. I haven't been brought up to sit at home doing nothing. I want to go back to work, prove that I can make my own way in the publishing world.' She had paused and then had forced herself to say what her mother had said to her. 'I shouldn't have married you when you asked me. I should have waited. You rushed me into it.'

He had gone very pale, but he hadn't argued with her any more. He hadn't pleaded with her, either, to return with him to Canada. After staring at her coldly and assessingly for a few moments he had said,

'Okay, I get the message. You want a separation. You can have it. Perhaps we both need time to find out if being married to each other is what we both really want.' His crooked grin had been brash, yet a little self-mocking too. 'I guess I did kind of rush you into it, didn't I?' he had remarked, giving the impression that he had been pleased with the manoeuvre as if their marriage had been a business take-over he had brought to a successful conclusion. 'You see, I had to. . . .' he had broken off abruptly and had chewed at the corner of his lower lip. Then he had shrugged and had given her another cold-eyed look. 'Our marriage achieved what I wanted at the time, so I'm not complaining. Do you agree, then, to a separation?'

'For how long?' Even now Samantha could remember how chilled she had been by his cool attitude.

'For as long as it take you to sort things out, I suppose, and find out what it is what you want out of life,' he had replied, and had turned away from her with another shrug. 'Would two years suit you?' he had queried.

Two years then had seemed to her to be nearly a lifetime stretching away from her, more than enough time for her to find out what it was she wanted.

'Yes,' she had replied in a cold, miserable little voice. 'But ... but we'll meet sometimes, won't we? You'll come and see me?'

Craig had turned to face her. Across the width of the room at her parents' home which they had shared while he had been visiting they had stared at each other. Seeing the cold implacability of his face, the wintriness of his eyes, Samantha had almost broken down, had almost rushed forward to fling her arms about him. She had almost given in and had said she would return with him to Canada. Only the memory of the tediousness of her way of life there, the dullness of long days spent by herself when he had been away from her, plus the memory of Morgana Taylor, had prevented her from moving.

'No, I think not,' he had replied crisply. 'It'll be best if we don't meet. I'll make arrangements to pay you a separation allowance. . . .'

And so it had been settled, and Craig had gone back to Canada without her, convincing her by his behaviour that he would be glad to be free of her for a while and return to the ways of a bachelor; free to go and come when he liked; free to enjoy dangerous pursuits like sky-diving and car-racing; free to play with Morgana.

Hurt more deeply than she would have cared to admit, Samantha had taken the job at *Woman's Insight*, determined to work hard and to prove herself, but she had missed Craig more than she would have believed possible. Several times she had written to him during the first year of their separation, but he had never replied to her letters. Pride had stepped in and she had stopped writing. The second year without him had been easier. Successful in her work she had begun to socialise more and had actually struck up a friendship with another man, Lyndon Barry, a journalist who wrote for the daily newspaper which was published in the same building as *Woman's Insight*.

She hadn't forgotten Craig. She had begun to realise ruefully that she would never forget him, perhaps because a woman never forgets her first serious love, but she had begun to accept too that perhaps he wasn't for her after all. She had begun to think about divorce, had in fact consulted a lawyer about how best to go about obtaining one, when the blow had fallen and she had been asked to resign from her job because *Woman's Insight* had been forced to cut back on editorial staff.

She had been trying rather unsuccessfully to find another job in publishing when she had received Carla's letter containing Howard Clifton's invitation. Fed up with the dreariness of wintertime in

England as well as with being unemployed, she had been intrigued by the invitation. On impulse she had accepted it, drawn some of the separation allowance that had been accumulating in her bank account, bought a return ticket to Antigua and some clothes suitable for wearing in the tropics and had come here.

And now she was wondering why she had come. Had she hoped subconsciously to meet Craig again? More than two years had gone by since they had separated, so it was time they discussed their situation.

'Do you come to this place often?'

Craig's voice, softened by amusement, spoke quite near to her. Startled out of her musings, realising that the backs of her legs and her shoulders were beginning to burn, Samantha raised her head and sat up quickly.

He was standing at her side, drops of water beading his suntanned skin and glinting in the sunlight, making him look as if he was covered in sequins. Behind him, pulled up on the sand beside hers, was the other windsurfer.

'How did you know I was here?' she exclaimed.

'I saw you leave the beach on the other side and decided to follow you,' he replied, sitting down beside her. 'I see you haven't forgotten how to windsurf,' he added softly. 'Remember the fun we had when you were learning how in the Bahamas?'

Their expression frankly sensual, his eyes looked right into her and a faint whimsical smile curved his lips as if to underline another meaning in what he had said; the implication that they had had fun also when she had been learning how to make love; a subtle hint at past, shared intimacy.

Something dark and quivering seemed to uncoil within her in response to the way he was looking at her, the stirring of physical desire. Excitement throbbed through her. He was there, close to her, seeming to radiate with sex appeal. She had only to move her hand a few inches and she would touch his hairy sinewy thigh, stroke it suggestively.

He lay back suddenly on the sand, stretching his legs before him and pillowing his head on his clasped hands.

'So here we are, sunbathing together after all, in spite of your excuse that you had other things to do,' he remarked dryly.

'But not for long,' she replied, springing to her feet. 'I've had enough sun. I'm going back.'

She started towards the surfboards, but something got in her way and she tripped and measured her length on the sand. Instantly Craig was beside her, a hand on her arm to help her up.

'What happened?' he asked.

'Oh, you know damned well what happened!' she seethed as she sat up again and shook his hand from her arm. 'You tripped me!'

Quickly she lunged to her feet, intending to run away from him into the water, but he was on his feet too, grabbing at her and catching her just as she reached the edge of the shore. Blindly she pushed hard against him and went dashing into the soft glinting sea, tripping again and losing her balance, floundering wildly as something caught hold of one of her legs. A hand. Craig's hand.

Under the water she sank, spluttering as she gasped, swallowing salt water. Strong arms went around her and she was lifted above the surface. He set her down on her feet and held her against

him so tightly she could feel the thrust of his
maleness against the lower part of her body.

Shaking back her wet hair, she looked up. The
glitter in his eyes seemed to menace her. There was
a sensual threat in the way his lips were parting as
they came closer to hers. Fighting as much against
the passion which was surging through her, urging
her to meet him halfway and offer her lips to his
kiss, she pushed against him again.

'No, Craig—no! I don't want to. I don't want
to!'

'Sure you do, darling. We both want to. It's
been a long time. Too long,' he murmured huskily,
and began to kiss her hungrily, searing her lips
with the heat of his, while his hands stroked her
back gently, suggestively.

It took a lot of effort, a lot of self-control not to
respond to that kiss, but she managed to keep still
and stiff and when he raised his head at last she
said tauntingly,

'You haven't changed much, have you? You still
think you can walk in and take over, even after
two years of separation, without a word of
explanation or discussion, without taking my
feelings or what I want to do into account. Please
let go of me. I want to go back now. I've had
enough of this place. You . . . you've spoiled it for
me by coming out here!'

He let go of her at once and she waded ashore
to prepare the windsurfer. She thought he might
follow her, but when she turned around to look he
was running out into the sea. Shading her eyes
against the glare of sunlight on water, Samantha
watched him dive beneath the surface. He
reappeared some way out in the bay to swim

strongly, glinting brown arms cleaving through the blue-green water.

Strong and silent. Samantha's lips curled in a wry grimace as she put the mast into its slot. Craig had always been a strong, silent lover, going straight for what he wanted. It had usually been what she had wanted too, until she had found out about Morgana.

'I'll race you back across the bay,' he challenged cheerfully, wading out of the sea, brown-skinned and powerful, apparently undisturbed by her rejection of his lovemaking, and she knew a certain discouragement. Never had she been able to get under his skin. Never had she been able to hurt him in the way he could hurt her.

'All right,' she agreed. 'But you'll have to give me a start. I'm not as good as you are on a windsurfer.'

Over the sun-dazzled flurries of tiny waves the windsurfer bobbed. In the attempt to go faster than Craig and to arrive at the opposite shore before he did Samantha took chances she wouldn't have taken normally, and twice when she was sailing too close to the wind the boom and sail swung over and knocked her off the board and into the water. Each time she capized Craig sailed close to her, shouted to ask her if she was all right and waited around until she was back on her board and sailing again.

As it happened, she reached the beach below Cliff House before he did, but she couldn't be sure whether it was because she had sailed faster than he had or whether he had held back to let her win. They carried the boards and masts and sails up to the racks under the shelter of the trees together.

'Are you going to see your father now?' asked Samantha, thinking she should remind him of his filial duty. 'Carla was upset because you didn't go straight to see him when you arrived at the house.'

'So she said,' he remarked coolly. His light eyes glinted wickedly in the shadow cast by the palm fronds as he slanted a glance at her. 'But you know me . . . or you should by now. First things first, always.'

'Meaning?' she queried.

'Meaning that now I've attended to the first thing, now that I've reminded you that you're still my wife and that I have the right to kiss you when I want, I'll go and see the old man and find out what it is he's got in mind,' he replied, stepping towards her.

Bending his head, he kissed her hard on the mouth before she could retort. But he didn't touch her anywhere else. She swayed under that unexpected passionate onslaught and this time couldn't control the response that leapt up like a dark flame within her. She would have caught hold of him to steady herself, but he stepped back quickly and turning on his heel walked away over the soft heaps of sand towards the steps.

CHAPTER THREE

SLOWLY Samantha followed Craig up the steps. Nothing had changed, she thought miserably. He hadn't changed. He still took her for granted and she was still at his mercy because he could turn her on. He could still arouse desire in her, make it flow through her like molten lava, red-hot, destroying all sensible thought, all opposition. Yet she was just as far from knowing whether he was in love with her as she had ever been.

How could she stay while he was at Cliff House and continue to resist him? She couldn't. She would be a nervous wreck if she stayed on. She would have to leave, no matter what arguments Carla put forward about her staying because Howard Clifton wanted her to stay and read to him. She couldn't stay and be treated as Craig treated her, like an item on an agenda for a board meeting of Clifton Enterprises.

Item 1. Remind Samantha that she is still the wife of Craig Clifton, vice-president, and that he still has the right to kiss her and make love to her when he feels like it.

Oh, no. She wasn't going to stay and be treated like that. She was leaving right now. She began to hurry along the path through the shrubbery. By the time she reached the house Craig had gone inside. In the hallway she came face to face with Farley, who was obviously on his way out. He was fully dressed now in bright pink cotton pants and a navy blue short-sleeved shirt.

'Why did you go off like that?' he demanded, scowling at her. 'Why didn't you stay and help me out like you promised?'

'I ... I'm sorry,' she muttered. She had forgotten all about her promise to help him explain to Craig why he didn't want to return to Harvard. Craig had appeared and she had become confused as usual, preoccupied only with her own reactions to him. 'What did he say?' she asked. 'Did he give you hell for wanting to drop out?'

'No, as a matter of fact he didn't,' said Farley, his scowl fading. 'He didn't seem to be at all interested in me. He said he didn't care what I wanted to do with my life because he had more important things on his mind. He said I could go to hell my own way as long as it didn't cost him anything.' Farley's lips twitched into a grin. 'And then he told my mother to shut up and stop complaining and walked off. I guess he followed you?'

'Yes, he did. So you're not going back to Harvard.'

'No. I'm going to Toronto as soon as I can get a seat on a plane. But right now I'm going down to the Dockyard, to the Admiral's Inn, to pick up the Taylors and bring them here for dinner.'

'The Taylors?' whispered Samantha, feeling a strange chill go through her.

'That's right. Conrad Taylor and his daughter Morgana. It seems they've flown out to visit Dad.' He began to walk towards the front doorway. 'See you,' he said.

'Farley, wait for me,' she said urgently, going after him. 'I ... I promised Pamela and Ken Wallis I'd meet them at the Inn. I'm going out to dinner with them, but I must change first. Please wait.'

'Okay. I'll be in the Caddy.'

Down the passageway to her suite of rooms Samantha hurried. From the bathroom came the sound of the shower and she guessed Craig was in there, getting rid of salt from his skin and hair. There was no time for her to do the same. Quickly she grabbed some clothes from the closet, jeans, shorts, a couple of shirts, a sweater, underwear from a drawer. She stuffed everything into a soft zipped holdall, grabbed her handbag, made sure her wallet and passport were in it, took off the sun-dress she was wearing and the *maillot*, dressed swiftly in clean underwear and another sun-dress, this time in white cotton splashed with coloured flowers, draped a cardigan around her shoulders, gave her still damp hair a quick flick with a comb and with the holdall slung over her shoulder ran from the room just as she heard the shower stop.

Farley was waiting in the Cadillac as he had promised, and although he gave her holdall a curious glance he didn't say anything. Soon they were speeding along the narrow road on their way back to Falmouth and on to English Harbour.

Farley parked the car in the parking lot outside Nelson's Dockyard and together they walked along the roadway to the narrow entrance. The women who always sold fresh island-grown vegetables as well as simple cotton sun-dresses which they had made in their own homes were packing up their wares and preparing to go home, but that didn't stop them from calling out to Samantha and Farley, inviting them to buy.

A chain across the narrow roadway prevented

vehicles from driving straight into the Dockyard and they had to pay a dollar each to go into the precincts, the money going to an organisation called the Society of the Friends of English Harbour which was responsible for restoration and upkeep of the old buildings.

After paying they turned abruptly to the left, passing the big stone pillars that were all that remained of one of the buildings, and walked into the garden terrace of the Admiral's Inn. The inn itself was a building of mellow brownish bricks which had been brought from England. It had been completed in 1788 and had been the offices of the Engineers of the Dockyard. Now it was a well-known hostelry and a meeting place for yachtsmen from all over the world.

Its terrace was one of Samantha's favourite places. Shaded by feathery casuarinas and overlooking the blue waters of the narrowest part of the harbour, it had an atmosphere of timeless serenity. Whenever she visited it she felt she could sit there for ever one one of the comfortable blue-cushioned couches, watching the play of sunlight on water, hearing the hum of pleasant conversation around her and occasionally taking a sip from a long cool drink.

'Over here!' called a voice from the corner of the terrace farthest away from the entrance, and a long bare arm waved.

'There's Pam,' Samantha explained to Farley. 'I expect you'll find the Taylors inside.'

'I guess so. When do you want to go back to Cliff House?'

'I'll find my own way back,' she replied. 'Later.'

'Okay.'

He went up the shallow steps in front of the building and disappeared through one of the three long open windows which led directly into the bar and lounge. Samantha made her way between the tables where people were sitting and drinking, to the table where Pamela Wallis was sitting on one of the couches.

'I was beginning to think you weren't coming,' said Pamela. A little older than Samantha, closer to thirty than to twenty, she was tall and had short brown sun-bleached hair. Her skin had been tanned to an even golden colour and she was dressed in very white shorts and a navy blue T-shirt with the name *Sylphide* printed in white letters on it. She came from the same town in Essex that Samantha came from and had gone to school with Samantha's elder sister Jennifer. Quite recently she and her husband Ken Wallis had sailed their forty-three-foot ketch *Sylphide* across the Atlantic from Falmouth, England, and had arrived in Falmouth, Antigua. They were on their way through the islands to the States and hoped to reach the coast of Maine by the month of July, when they would join in a celebration of the Cruising Club of America's Eastern Station's sixtieth birthday, to which Cruising clubs from Great Britain and from Ireland had been invited to participate.

Samantha had met and recognised Pamela several days before when she had been wandering around the dockyard's museum, and since then, delighted to find someone familiar so far from England, she had managed to meet her every day.

'I had to go to the airport to meet someone,' Samantha replied, sitting down on the couch. 'Isn't Ken ashore with you?'

'I left him at the yacht chandlers,' replied Pam. 'Who was that young man who came in with you?' she asked curiously.

'Farley Clifton.'

'Not your husband, surely?'

'Oh, no. Farley is Craig's half-brother.' Samantha paused, wondering how much she should tell Pamela.

'What is it, Samantha? What's bothering you? You seem to be all het up about something?' Pamela asked quietly. 'You can tell me, you know. I can promise you it won't go any further.'

'Craig arrived today. I . . . I had to go and meet him at the airport,' replied Samantha abruptly. 'He . . . I . . . well, we've been separated for two years and . . .' She broke off, making a helpless gesture with her hands. 'I can't stay while he's at Cliff House. I'll have to leave. Are you still thinking of sailing to Nevis tomorrow?'

'We are. And the invitation to you to come with us is still open,' said Pamela. Her glance went to Samantha's holdall. 'I notice you've a bag with you. Does that mean you're going to come aboard with us after dinner and stay for the night so we can make an early start tomorrow morning?'

'That's right, if you're sure I won't be too much trouble—be in the way,'

'We wouldn't have invited you if we'd thought that. We'll enjoy your company. You can come all the way with us, if you like; all the way to Maine.'

'Oh no, I couldn't do that. I'll have to get off somewhere and fly back to London some time. Just as long as I can get away from here as soon as possible,' said Samantha. 'Thanks, Pam.'

'Don't mention it,' Pamela smiled. 'You know I

still can't get over our meeting in the museum the other day, thousands of miles away from Epping.' She looked past Samantha whose back was to the inn building. 'Your half brother-in-law is coming this way and has someone with him,' she added in a low voice.

Samantha looked over her shoulder. Farley was approaching and he was followed by a woman; a tall woman with white blonde curls that glittered like tinsel in the sunlight; a white-skinned woman whose dark eyes were hidden by sun-glasses and who was dressed in a sleek blue linen pant suit and had a blue straw hat tilted rakishly on her head. Morgana Taylor.

'Samantha, how nice to see you.' Morgana showed perfect teeth and held out a hand. Gold bracelets clashed together on her thin wrist. 'I'd no idea you'd be in Antigua too.'

Samantha touched the held-out hand briefly, withdrawing her own hand quickly. Shaking hands with Morgana was like taking hold of a limp lettuce leaf.

'Where are you staying?' Morgana went on.

'I . . . I've been staying at Cliff House,' replied Samantha stiffly. 'Have you come for a holiday?'

'Well, not exactly. I came with Father. He wants to see Howard, about something to do with business, and I knew Craig would be here, so I jumped at the chance to come when Daddy asked me to accompany him. I'm hoping too to do some research for a new novel I have in mind.' She glanced at Pamela and smiled. 'I'm a writer,' she explained. 'Novels about the modern woman, you know. The feminist movement and how it has affected our life-styles. Perhaps you've read one of my books. The name is Morgana Taylor.'

'No, I don't think I have,' replied Pamela, rising to her feet. 'There's Ken now, Samantha,' she added. 'Are you ready to go to the yacht?'

'Aren't you coming to Cliff House?' asked Morgana sharply.

'No. I'm going away for a few days with Pam and her husband, on their yacht,' replied Samantha. 'Goodbye, Morgana. Have a good stay on the island. Goodbye, Farley. Please tell Carla I'll be writing to her.'

'Hey, wait a minute!' called Farley after her as she followed Pamela to the steps in front of the hotel where Ken was waiting for them. 'Wait, Sam! Tell me, when are you coming back from your cruise?'

'I'm not,' she replied.

'But you can't just go off like this, without telling anyone where you're going,' objected Farley.

'I'm telling you, aren't I?' she retorted. 'And why can't I go where I please when I want to? It's all right, Farley—honestly,' she added, turning to him as they reached the steps in front of the hotel. 'I'm not going away with strangers. Come and meet Pam and Ken. Once you've met them you'll know I'll be quite safe going with them. Pam happens to be a friend of my sister's and I've known her for years.'

Farley shook hands politely with the Wallises and Pamela assured him that they were looking forward to having Samantha on board for a few days.

'Do you know exactly which islands you'll be visiting?' Farley asked causally.

'Nevis first and then maybe St Bart's and Anguilla. We're hoping to go through the British

Virgins and on to St Thomas in the American Virgins,' said Ken affably.

'Will you go that far?' Farley asked Samantha. Behind him on the steps Morgana had been joined by a tall grey-haired man who was presumably Conrad Taylor.

'I'm not sure. When I've had enough I'll get off wherever there's an airport where I can catch a flight directly to England or, failing that, to Miami.'

'Then you won't be coming back here,' exclaimed Farley, looking very puzzled.

'No.'

'But what about Craig?' he whispered, after giving a wary glance at the Wallises.

'What about him?' replied Samantha coolly.

'He's come to Antigua to see you. I know he has, because Mother told me.'

'I don't believe he's come only to see me,' said Samantha in a low voice, noticing that Morgana was approaching them. 'I think he's come because he knew Morgana would be here.'

'Morgana?' repeated Farley, looking even more puzzled. 'Why would he want to see her? He can see her any time he wants in Toronto. Although I can't understand why he would want to, she's such a bore, going on about her writing all the time. To hear her talk you'd think she'd written *the* great Canadian novel of the twentieth century!'

'She and Craig have always had something going between them, and that's all I can say now,' whispered Samantha. 'Anyway, don't worry about it, Farley. I know what I'm doing. Please tell Carla that if she's upset because I've left in such a hurry.' Aware that the Wallises were strolling away and that Morgana and her father were coming closer, she reached up and kissed Farley on the cheek. 'I must go,' she murmured. 'Goodbye, Farley. And good luck with your new career.'

Through the dockyard Samantha hurried after the Wallises, past old buildings, their bricks glowing in the mellow golden light of late afternoon; past a row of old wooden capstans, painted black and white, relics of the time when ships of the Royal Navy had been hauled out of the water at the dockyard to have the keels careened, the growth of weed and barnacles that had formed on their bottoms during weeks and months in the salt water being scraped away. Warm wind swayed the fronds of palm trees clustering around the museum, once known as the Admiral's House, a wooden building painted white with grey shutters edging its long windows and an elegant verandah with wooden railings built out over the windows to give them shade from the hot bright sun which supported a balcony outside the upper windows.

At the wharf behind the restored Officers' Quarters John Wallis, Ken's younger brother, who had flown out from England to join Pam and Ken for their cruise through the islands, was waiting for them. They all stepped into the *Zodiac*, the big rubber dinghy powered by an outboard engine which the Wallises used as a tender to their yacht, and in a few seconds were zooming over the calm gold glinting water, weaving between the many moored yachts towards the two-masted, broad-beamed *Sylphide*.

The sun set and after a brief twilight, darkness came, a blue-black cloak studded with the diamond-like stars and the yellow gleam of shore-lights. Leaving the yacht again, they went in the *Zodiac* to the nearest shore to dine in an open-air restaurant with the crew of another British yacht, returning to *Sylphide* soon after ten o'clock to go to bed so that they could be up early next day.

So far so good, Samantha thought as she lay in the bunk in the fore-cabin of the yacht listening to the wind sighing in the rigging, the occasional rattle of the anchor chain as the boat swung and watching the stars swing by through the open hatchway above her. She had escaped. Farley would tell Carla where she had gone and Craig would get the message too, and surely it would become clear to him at last that their marriage was over.

She turned restlessly, recalling what he had said during the drive out to Cliff House from the airport. *He had always hoped they would get together again when she had stopped behaving like a spoiled child.* He didn't want a divorce.

Divorce. Divorce. The hateful word seemed to pound through her brain. Divorcing Craig had seemed to be the right course of action when she had been in England and hadn't seen or heard from him for two years. But now, after seeing him again, after having felt passion surge through her in reaction to his touch, she wondered about herself. Was it possible she was still in love with him?

She fell asleep with the question still shaping itself in her mind, and towards morning she dreamed she was with Craig, swimming with him, walking with him, hand in hand, along a deserted beach on a deserted island, as they had walked so often on their honeymoon. And she was happy because she was with him. She could feel the happiness bubbling up within her, even in the dream. She was happy because she had him to herself. There were no business meetings, no business trips abroad to take him away from her. Above all there was no Morgana Taylor.

But quite suddenly he dropped her and went running off into the wide sunlit sea, diving under the surface, and not coming up. Frantically she searched the shining expanse of water for a sight of his dark head and his brown arms, but he didn't reappear and she was crying to him to come back to her. *Come back, Craig. Come back to me!*

'Samantha—time to get up! We're leaving now.'

Pamela's voice broke through the dream and Samantha woke up to find her friend looking down at her, amusement twinkling in her hazel eyes.

'That was quite a dream you were having,' Pamela remarked. 'You were muttering and twisting about.'

'It wasn't very nice,' said Samantha with a grimace. 'I'm glad you woke me up.'

'It's a beautiful morning,' said Pamela. 'The wind is just right and Ken says we should be in Nevis by late afternoon. When you're dressed come through to the cockpit for coffee and rolls.'

She left the cabin and the boat shuddered slightly as the engine was started. Overhead on the deck Samantha heard footsteps and guessed John had come forward to cast off the mooring line.

In the cockpit Ken was steering, standing behind the compass pedestal to which the big wheel was attached. Short and stocky, his crest of brownish sun-bleached hair well brushed, his reddish brown beard neatly trimmed and with sun-glasses covering his eyes, he was looking ahead and altering course every so often to avoid other yachts as he steered *Sylphide* towards the narrow opening of the harbour and the wide shining sea beyond it.

'Nice-looking craft coming up on the port side,' he said to Samantha as she sat down in a corner of the cockpit, under the blue canvas dodger that curved over the entrance to the cabin. 'It's about the same size as this but is more rakish about the bow. My, she's a beauty! Well kept too. Just look at the shine on that varnishwork!'

Samantha looked over at the yacht they were passing. Dark blue hull and a varnished wooden deckhouse; two glinting golden masts; dark red sail covers. She recognised the yacht only too well. It was *Blue Falcon*, Howard Clifton's ketch, the boat she had cruised on with Craig in the Bahamas. Her lips tightened as she suppressed a surge of sadness. What happy times she had known on that yacht; times she had believed she would never forget; times she hadn't forgotten, she realised miserably.

'Do you know who owns it?' She became aware that Ken was speaking to her again and she looked at him, away from *Blue Falcon*'s pointed bow.

'It belongs to Howard Clifton,' she replied stiffly.

'Any relation to you?' Ken queried.

'Only ... only by marriage,' she muttered. Apparently Pamela hadn't told her husband anything that Samantha had told her about herself. 'He's ... he's my father-in-law,' she added.

'He wouldn't be the Howard Clifton who owns newspapers in Canada and in England and is a multi-millionaire, would he?' asked John Wallis curiously. He had returned to the cockpit and was sitting in the corner opposite to Samantha.

'That's right,' agreed Samantha, and was glad that Pamela had appeared with a tray of coffee mugs. 'He's president and chairman of Clifton Enterprises.'

'Thought so,' said John. 'I was hearing in the bar at the Admiral's Inn the other day that Conrad Taylor is hoping to take over Clifton Enterprises. In fact the person who told me pointed Taylor out to me. He's staying at the Inn right now with his daughter.' John grinned at her as he reached for a mug of coffee. 'It meant nothing much to me, but I guess it does to you. I suppose you know all about the take-over bid.'

'No, I didn't know until you told me,' she replied stiffly. 'They ... the Cliftons, I mean ... don't talk about the business to me.'

Much to Samantha's relief Pamela began to talk about something else and the Cliftons and the Taylors were forgotten, and by the time they had all finished drinking coffee and eating fresh rolls stuffed with chopped ham, the boat had left the harbour and was rolling and pitching over the swell of the sea.

The sails were hoisted, the engine was turned off and the strong steady trade wind filled the triangles of shimmering white terylene. The yacht leapt forward, heeling a little to the port side.

'We'll be able to reach all the way to Nevis with the wind in this quarter. No need to tack or pull in the sheets,' said Ken. 'Easy sailing all the way today and nothing much to do except sunbathe and sleep.'

After helping Pamela to clear away the remains of breakfast Samantha went on to the foredeck and sat in front of the mainmast in the shade provided by the shadow of the mast and the big mainsail. In front of her the two foresails billowed and swayed as the yacht rolled from side to side over the waves, and framed by their curves, in the space that separated them, she could see the shape of an island, its hills misty purple against a sky of pure unwavering blue. Montserrat, thirty-five miles away and known as the Garden Island. Looking the other way, to windward, she could see no signs of land, only the heaving, glittering dark blue sea, stretching away to a boundless horizon. Looking up, she watched for a few moments the sunlit tip of the mast and the gilded triangle of the mainsail swinging back and forth under the blue arch of the sky.

Samantha had changed position, was lying with her legs in a patch of sunlight beyond the shadow of the mast and with her head and shoulders propped against a sailbag, full of sail, which acted as a bolster and which was tied to the mainmast, when Pamela came to join her and to offer a long cold glass of fruit juices mixed with coconut milk as 'elevenses'.

'You seem to have found a good place to avoid the heat of the sun,' she remarked as she sat down. 'The cockpit gets too hot when the sun is behind us. How do you like *Sylphide*?'

'She's very comfortable.'

'As comfortable as Howard Clifton's yacht? I presume you've sailed on that at some time or other,' said Pamela, probing, but ever so gently.

'Yes, I have. *Sylphide* is wider and perhaps not so fast as *Blue Falcon*,' Samantha replied.

There was a short silence while they both sipped their drinks. The icy pineapple, orange and coconut-flavoured bubbles tingled against Samantha's parched throat, easing her thirst.

'I hate asking anyone about their personal lives,' said Pamela, leaning back against the sail bag and tilting her head so that she could look up at the mast swinging back and forth, 'but I am puzzled about you. If I asked you why you'd separated from your husband, would you tell me?'

'Yes,' said Samantha. 'I've nothing to hide. I just decided one day that I couldn't go back to Toronto and live the sort of life the wife of a wealthy business executive is expected to live. I decided I wanted to continue with my career in London. Craig didn't like my decision and suggested we separated for a couple of years to find out if marriage to each other was what we both really wanted.' She paused, then added in a low voice, 'Yesterday we met for the first time in two years.'

'And?'

'He . . . he behaved as if the separation is over and we can get together again.'

'But you don't feel the same way?'

'Nothing has changed,' muttered Samantha. 'He . . . he isn't in love with me any more than he was when we got married. I'm still only an item on a business agenda to him, to be fitted in between other items that are more important. Such as take-over bids, reorganising Clifton Enterprises, making money,' she added with a touch of bitterness. 'And then there's always Morgana Taylor.'

'Oh, the weird novelist we met at the Admiral's Inn,' remarked Pam with a mocking little laugh.

'She was really something else, wasn't she? The complete female egotist—worse than the male variety. What has she to do with your husband?'

'He's known her for years. And I think she's his mistress,' said Samantha flatly.

'My God!' Pamela rolled her eyes comically. 'How on earth did a nice well-brought-up English girl like you get involved with such kinky people?' Her glance at Samantha was shrewd. 'But I think I begin to understand why you wanted to come on this cruise with us. You couldn't stay around in Antigua while the Taylor woman is there, knowing how things are between her and Craig. Right?'

'Right. Although I'd more or less decided I couldn't stay at Cliff House while Craig was there before I'd heard Morgana had come to the island.'

'You're afraid of him?' exclaimed Pamela.

'Yes, in a way,' Samantha admitted.

'M God!' breathed Pamela again. 'He hasn't . . . surely he hasn't . . .?' Words seemed to fail her as she stared at Samantha, her hazel eyes round and horrified in the shadow cast by the brim of her white linen sun-hat. 'He hasn't beaten you or . . . or raped you or anything like that, has he?' she added in a whisper.

'Oh no.' Samantha couldn't help smiling at her friend's expression of horror. 'Perhaps I've given you the wrong impression. I'm not exactly afraid of anything Craig does . . . to me,' she continued, frowning as she tried to express herself more clearly. 'I'm . . . just afraid of being in the same house that he is, in the same room.'

'I see,' Pamela nodded in understanding, the expression of horror fading from her face, giving way to one of sympathy. 'Oh, I see very well.

You're not afraid of him—you're afraid of your own reactions to him. You're afraid of the emotions being near him arouses in you.' She slanted another shrewd glance at Samantha. 'Sounds to me as if you're still in love with him and you're angry with yourself for feeling like that about a man who regards you as an item on a business meeting agenda. It's yourself you're running away from, not him, isn't it?'

'I suppose so,' muttered Samantha miserably, facing up to the truth about herself. 'Oh, Pam, I thought it would be so different when I agreed to marry him. I thought we'd be together all the time and share everything.'

'Mmm, you certainly had great expectations, didn't you?' drawled Pamela dryly. 'And how long did you give your marriage? Eighteen months? A whole year and a half? Hardly a fair trial, Samantha.'

'Mother says I shouldn't have married when I did. She says I was too young. Immature was the word she used, actually,' said Samantha.

'I can imagine,' said Pam. 'Mrs Lewis is nothing if not forthright. But she was probably right about you. Never mind, Sam,' she went on, patting Samantha's arm. 'You've made your move. The next one is up to Craig. I suppose someone will tell him where you've gone?'

'Farley will. But I'm not expecting Craig to do anything. I'm not expecting anything from him at all. Not any more,' replied Samantha with a sigh.

Pamela made no reply this time, but the expression in her eyes was anxious as she studied Samantha's profile. After a while she stood up.

'Come on,' she said breezily. 'Let's go and

relieve Ken and John. You can steer the ship while I keep a lookout.' She looked around. 'Mmm, we're belting along at a fair rate of knots. I can hardly see Antigua now and Montserrat is fast disappearing into the blue too. I wonder how long before we'll see Nevis?'

Nevis appeared on the horizon in the middle of the afternoon, a high misty blue cone-shaped mountain, its top seeming to be covered with snow. As *Sylphide* rolled nearer the illusion of snow became a cream-puff of cloud hovering above sloping green and yellow fields and scattered trees. By the time the sun was setting, flushing the western sky with crimson and gold, the yacht was anchored among other yachts a few miles offshore in the roadstead at Charlestown, the capital of Nevis.

Next morning they went ashore in the *Zodiac* to report to the Customs and Immigration offices and then took a taxi ride around the beautiful island.

First they visited the deserted remains of the Bath Hotel, an elegant stone building, situated near a pool of curative waters and dating from the eighteenth century. It had been built to receive visitors not only from the neighbouring islands but also from England who came to take the waters for the relief of varying afflictions, from gout to leprosy. From the hotel they drove on along a winding country road hedged by overgrown palms and flowering vines to St John's Church in Fig Tree village, a charming old building which looked as if it had just been transported from a Cornish village. Inside the walls were painted white and the wooden pillars were blue. The simple wooden pews glowed in the sunlight. Under a memorial plaque there was a battered register of marriages, open at a tattered page. Samantha bent over it and read an entry written in ink that had long been faded: '*1787, March 11, Horatio Nelson Esquire, Captain of His Majesty's Ship* Boreas, to *Frances Herbert Nesbit, Widow.*'

'She lived on one of the sugar plantations,' said Pamela, 'and the marriage took place at the Montpelier Estate, which is a hotel now. We're going there next.'

Rain was sweeping the island when at last they returned from the taxi drive and the visits to the various sugar plantations, all of them now converted into private hotels, and the wind was whipping the water in the roadstead into white-crested peaks. *Sylphide* was rolling and pitching at anchor, obviously unhappy, so Ken decided to move the yacht to a wide bay at the tip of St Kitts, the neighbouring island. As they were leaving the anchorage they noticed another yacht, its mainsail reefed down, a storm jib rigged on its forestay, entering the roadstead.

'Looks as if he's had a pretty rough passage,' remarked Ken. 'Have a look at him through the binoculars, John. See if it's anyone we know.'

It was a few minutes before John reported his findings. Since *Sylphide* was rocking and rolling rather violently under engine and without any sails up to steady her it took him some time to steady the binoculars and get a good look at the other yacht.

'Looks like that blue ketch from English Harbour,' he said at last. 'Although it could be another yacht just like it. Impossible for me to read the name at this distance.'

'You mean the one called *Blue Falcon*?' asked Ken.

'That's right.'

Samantha and Pamela looked at one another across the cockpit. Pamela's eyebrows lifted questioningly. Samantha looked away across the wind-tossed heaving grey water at the blue yacht, small now in the distance, looking no bigger than a dinghy as it heeled under a particularly strong gust of wind that swept down from the slopes of the cloud-capped, forest-clad Nevis Peak.

Was it *Blue Falcon*? Samantha felt excitement unfold within her and beat through her blood. And if it was Howard Clifton's yacht who was sailing her? It was an effort to keep her imagination under control, to stop it from winging across the wild waters to that distant yacht and seeing Craig at its wheel peering through the increasing grey murk brought by the rain and wind, searching for a place to anchor. It was difficult not to wonder who was with him on the yacht if it was Craig, to imagine that Morgana was with him, sharing the violence of the storm with him, helping him to sail the yacht.

But she mustn't let herself imagine Craig was so near, only a few miles away. She mustn't. To do that was to have expectations where he was concerned; to expect too much of him. And she didn't expect anything from him. Not any more.

Soon after *Sylphide* had been anchored in the wide Majors Bay at the tip of St Kitts darkness fell abruptly and rain drummed down, driving them below to spend the evening dining on the delicious meal of fresh fish and tropical fruits which Pamela had bought in the market at Charlestown, playing

cards and listening to the cassette tapes of music
that John had brought with him from England.
The night passed peacefully and the next morning
dawned fine and calm. After breakfast the anchor
was winched up, the engine was started and the
yacht motored out of the bay towards the narrow
strait which separates St Kitts from Nevis. Clouds
still hovered over Nevis Peak, but the sun climbing
fast in the blue sky shone brilliantly on the sea,
turning each white crest to silver.

Once they were through the dangerous rock-
strewn waters of the strait John hoisted the sails.
Again the wind was on the beam, not as strong as
it had been the day they had sailed from Antigua,
but steady, and Ken predicted that they would be
in St Barts, forty miles away, by early afternoon.

Close to the coast of the green island of St Kitts
they sailed. Behind them Nevis changed colour
from tawny green to misty purple, still wearing its
tiara of creamy clouds. Further and further away
from it, *Sylphide* sailed until it looked merely like a
blue triangle drawn by a child on bright blue
paper, thought Samantha as she stared back the
way they had come.

Just then something flickered in that blue
distance, something white, silvered by the bright
sunlight. Another sail? Another yacht, following
them?

'Don't look now,' John sang out mockingly,
'but I think we're being followed!' One arm
around the mizzenmast to steady himself, he was
standing precariously on the after coaming of the
cockpit and was peering through the binoculars
back the way they had come.

'Is it the blue ketch? The one we saw sailing into

Charlestown last evening?' asked Pamela, voicing the question which sprang immediately into Samantha's mind.

'No, I don't think so,' drawled John staring intently through the glasses. 'It isn't heeling enough to be a single hull and it's moving like a fiend out of hell in this wind. It's a trimaran—yes, that's what it is, and at the rate it's going it will soon overtake us. No sign of the blue ketch.'

Samantha felt the tension which had tightened her nerves ease a little and determinedly she turned her back on the islands of Nevis and St Kitts and looked forward, searching the horizon ahead of *Sylphide*'s bow for other islands. Not once did she look back during the rest of that day of blue and gold, but always she had the feeling that she wanted to look over her shoulder to see if the blue ketch was following them.

CHAPTER FOUR

LEAVING *Sylphide* anchored in a wide bay at the entrance to the harbour of Gustavia, the capital city of the French island of St Barthelemy—known affectionately as St Barts—the Wallises and Samantha went into the harbour in the *Zodiac*, glad of its size and speed for the long ride.

Under the hot and brilliant sunshine of midday the softly weathered roofs of the town glowed the colour of geranium flowers against the vivid green hills surrounding the harbour which was crowded with many yachts as well as with old trading schooners and other freighters, loading and unloading at the town wharves.

Originally settled as long ago as 1645 by fishermen from Normandy and Brittany, St Barts had been ceded by the French to Sweden in 1784 in return for trading rights and, for almost a century, the island had been an outpost of Sweden far away from the islands of the Baltic sea, and although it had been sold back to France in 1877 traces of Scandinavian influence remained in the small windows and decorative scrollwork on many of the houses as well as in the name of the capital town.

But now the French influence was predominant. The people spoke in French. The cars moving in an apparently endless stream through the narrow streets of the town were French. At the corner where two streets met two French *gendarmes* stood talking, immaculate in pale khaki shorts and shirts, peaked caps and knee socks. The shops featured French perfumes, crystal and jewellery and other French luxury items.

After lunching at a harbourside café Samantha and Pamela decided they wanted to explore the rest of the island while Ken and John shopped for yacht chandlery, so after arranging with the two men to meet them at sunset on the terrace of a well-known hotel restaurant on a hillside overlooking the harbour, they rented a small car and set off.

The road twisted up a steep hill past the gardens of houses overflowing with flowering vines and shrubs. Down in the long inlet the water seemed to change colour as they went higher. A fleet of dinghies, taking part in a yacht club race, their sails many different colours, fluttered across the inlet in a light breeze.

At a place where a stone cross had been built on the hillside the road turned back on itself, threading through the thick green vegetation. Arriving at a fork in the road they turned right to drive past fences made from stones gathered from the land, the remains of the days when the area had been intensely cultivated, producing sugar and cotton and tobacco.

At Corossal Bay they lingered in the village that could have been lifted bodily from the coast of Brittany. Some of the women villagers, although going barefoot in that warm climate, wore the traditional pleated and frilled bonnets that their ancestors had introduced from France, long ago.

In a house behind a clump of low palms whose fronds, dried for two weeks in the sun after cutting, formed the material for woven hats, baskets and mats, Pamela and Samantha watched a group of women weaving hats. The floor of the living-room-workshop was made of pine and had been highly polished by generations of bare feet passing over it. A flowered curtain hung over the entrance to the bedroom. In a corner dangled a hammock. Chickens wandered in and out of the room. Children with fair skins and blue eyes peeped in through the unscreened, unglassed, uncurtained windows curious about the visitors. Behind their blond heads waved the scarlet blossoms of hibiscus.

After buying two of the hats that had wide turned-up brims and low crowns Samantha and Pamela drove back the way they had come and followed the left fork in the road that curved beside Baie de la Sainte Jeanne. Finding a crescent-shaped beach, fringed with palms, they swam for a while before driving on to look at the villages on the eastern rocky coast.

The sun was setting when they returned to Gustavia and drove up another steep hillside to the hotel where they had arranged to meet Ken and John. The two men were already on the open-air terrace drinking Planter's Punches. From the edge of the terrace there was a panoramic view of the harbour and the many yachts and freighters. The water was a pool of gold and the embracing arms of the land were purple, scattered with twinkling yellow lights. The heat of the day still lingered in the air, as did the scents of many flowers growing in the hillside gardens.

'I think I can just see *Sylphide* from here,' said Pamela. 'There seems to be another yacht anchored quite close to her.'

'The blue ketch,' replied Ken. 'It was just coming in when John and I went aboard this afternoon with the things we'd bought.'

'Did you see who was sailing it?' asked Samantha, trying to sound casual, as if she wasn't really all that interested; as if every nerve in her body wasn't suddenly tingling.

'A big fellow, well tanned,' replied Ken. 'He seemed to be on his own.'

'Did you speak to him?' asked Pamela.

'No. And he didn't speak to us. He was too busy anchoring and furling his sails,' said John. 'But the ketch is the *Blue Falcon* from the English Harbour.'

Samantha looked over the vine-entwined trellis to the outer part of the harbour, but it was impossible for her to see the shape of *Sylphide* now because the light had faded from the sky and the water and in the short tropical dusk the distant yachts had blended with the dark background of the land behind them.

But later, after a gourmet dinner in the elegant dining room of the hotel, when they all returned to *Sylphide* she saw *Blue Falcon*, three boat lengths away, lying quite still to the anchor line on the smooth light-reflecting water. The windows of the cabin glinted and the smooth varnishwork gleamed under the pale rays of the riding lights shining down from the spreaders of the mainmast. But there was no sign of anyone being on board.

Next morning the blue boat was still there, quiet and apparently deserted, perfectly reflected in the clear green water, when Samantha joined John in the *Zodiac* to go to the town to buy fresh French bread and croissants from the bakery.

A big fellow, well tanned. Oh, she had no doubt that Craig was on the sleek blue boat; that he had slept that night only a few yards away from her, the knowledge of his nearness tormenting during the times she had woken up. But why had he come? What was he doing here in Gustavia? Why hadn't he stayed in Antigua? Was he really following her? Or was it just a coincidence that he had anchored so close to *Sylphide*?

At that early hour of the morning the narrow streets of the town were quiet and the air was cool and fresh. Following their noses, which had quickly scented the wholesome smell of baking bread, they soon found a bakery. They bought several long loaves and two dozen croissants still hot from the oven, knowing that both bread and croissants would keep for a while, if well wrapped up, in the yacht's refrigerator.

Their shopping done, they walked back to the wharf where they had tied up the *Zodiac* at the bottom of some steps. A man was coming up the steps, a big fellow, well tanned, who had straight black hair. He was dressed in a white short-sleeved T-shirt moulded closely to his heavily-muscled chest and revealing his sinewy teak-coloured arms. About to go down the steps, her arms full of French loaves, Samantha stepped back quickly and looked around rather wildly as if searching for a place to run to and hide in.

'Hello, Samantha.' Craig spoke coolly and without surprise as if he had known all along that he would meet her at that particular place at that particular time, on Gustavia's town wharf not far from an old two-masted trading schooner loaded with, of all things, wooden cargo containers. 'I see you've found a bakery,' he drawled, taking off his sunglasses and looking at her appraisingly with slitted grey eyes. 'Is it far from here? That bread smells good.'

The sudden encounter had scattered her wits and she couldn't think how best to describe the way to the bakery. Her mouth and lips were dry and through her thin T-shirt the hot bread, clutched against her chest, was warming her up. The smell of it was strong in her nostrils. All she could do was stare at Craig, not knowing what to say, every nerve in her body tinglingly aware of his powerful presence, of the brown sheen of his tanned skin, of the glint in his light eyes, of the shapeliness of his muscular legs below the edge of his navy blue shorts. Vaguely she realised that John was giving him the directions to the bakery.

'Thanks,' said Craig, nodding at John, and he held out his right hand. 'I'm Craig Clifton, off *Blue Falcon.*'

'John Wallis.' John shook Craig's offered hand. 'We noticed you yesterday when you came in. You were at Charlestown on Nevis too, weren't you?'

'That's right.' Craig frowned and glanced sideways at Samantha, still silent and unable to go on her way down the steps to the *Zodiac* because she couldn't get past him. 'I didn't see you there, though,' he added, looking back at John.

'We went over to Major's Bay for that night. It wasn't very comfortable in the Charlestown anchorage.'

'You can say that again,' replied Craig with a grin. '*Blue Falcon* rolled like a pig all night and I'd had a pretty rough ride up from English Harbour that day, reefed right down. I was glad to be here last night to get a good sleep. Are you leaving here today?'

'After breakfast.'

'Going far?'

'Over to the French side of St Martin's island, to a place called Pinel's Key. There's good shelter there.'

'I know it,' said Craig, nodding again. 'There's good swimming and diving there too. I'll probably see you there.' With another nod at John and another sidelong glance at Samantha he walked away towards the town.

'Is he the Clifton you're married to?' asked John as he followed Samantha down the steps to the *Zodiac*.

'Yes.' She felt hot and bothered. Sweat was pricking her skin and her heart was thumping loudly in her ears.

'Do you think he's followed you here?'

'I don't know,' she replied, getting into the rubber boat and settling herself at the bow.

'It's a bit of a coincidence him turning up here if he hasn't,' John remarked dryly, and pressed the starter of the outboard motor. The engine roared and, glad that both noise and distance made any further conversation difficult, Samantha looked away from him and over the bow, feeling drops of spray borne on the rushing air cool her hot skin.

'Did you see him?' Pamela queried. She was in the neat L-shaped galley of the yacht lighting a burner on the propane gas cooker to boil water for coffee when Samantha dropped down the companionway with the bread and croissants. 'He left his boat soon after you and John went to the town.'

'Yes, we saw him. We met him just as he was going ashore and we were leaving.' Samantha put the bags she was carrying down on the counter.

'What did he say to you?' Pamela's glance was curious.

'Only hello.'

'So what did you say to him?'

'Nothing. Shall I slice this pineapple for you?'

'Yes, please.' Pamela opened a drawer and took out a big sharp knife and handed it to Samantha. 'Didn't you say hello too?'

'No. I ... I couldn't say anything.' Picking up the knife, Samantha began to cut through the greenish-yellow horny outside of the fruit, slicing off the top with its spiky, serrated leaves. 'He told John he would probably see us at Pinel's Key.' She cut more slices from the pineapple, Pam, do you know if I could get to the airport near Phillipsburg from Pinel's?'

'I don't think you could, not unless you had a car. It's a pretty remote place, judging by the chart, and most people go to it by boat.' Pamela was setting the table in the main part of the cabin and she turned round to look at Samantha. 'Why? Are you thinking of leaving us?'

'I thought I would if we go anywhere near an airport. Do you know where Ken intends to go from Pinel's?'

'He did say something about sailing across to Anguilla and spending a couple of days there. An old school chum of his owns a hotel on the island.'

Pamela returned to the galley and began to pour boiling water into the coffee maker. When she had done that she turned and leaned against the counter beside Samantha.

'You're all het up again, aren't you, because you've seen him,' she murmured, watching Samantha trying to cut off the hard pieces of skin clinging to the outside of one of the pale juicy slices of pineapple.

'I didn't think he would follow me,' Samantha muttered. 'I don't know why he's followed me.'

'Oh, come on,' Pamela mocked. 'Of course you know why he's followed you. He wants to see you and talk to you. And you can't go on running away from him for ever, you know. If he does follow us to Pinel's I'll ask him to come and have dinner with us.'

'Oh, no!' Samantha looked up from what she was doing and stared at her friend's comely suntanned face. 'Please don't, Pam. It will be so embarrassing if you do.'

'Embarrassing for whom?' queried Pamela, lifting finely plucked eyebrows. 'If you're worried about Ken or John or me being embarrassed just because you and Craig have been separated for two years and haven't got together again, forget it. We won't be. Too many couples we know back home have split up and yet we're still friendly with both parties and enjoy their company. As far as we're concerned Craig is a fellow yachtsman who probably has some interesting yarns about sailing to swap with us and who might have some useful information and advice about sailing among these islands to pass on to us. We won't be embarrassed by his company.'

Samantha didn't say anything but went on cutting up the slices of pineapple into chunks.

'Besides, I'd like to meet a man who'd sail his yacht single-handed through a storm like we had the other day just to catch up with his wife,' Pamela continued, then paused again as if to give Samantha a chance to say something, but Samantha stayed stubbornly silent, doggedly intent on finishing the preparation of the pineapple. 'But if it's going to embarrass you having dinner with him you can always go ashore while he's here. Or you could even get yourself invited on to another yacht,' Pamela went on. 'From what I've read about Pinel's it seems to be the perfect tropical paradise—beautiful beaches, shady palm trees, clear deep water far away from habitation, so there are bound to be other yachts there.'

'I still wish you wouldn't invite Craig,' muttered Samantha. 'I . . . I don't want to see him. I don't want to have anything to do with him,' she added vehemently. 'That's why I came away with you, but I didn't think he would follow me. Oh, please, Pam, don't invite him to come aboard this evening. Please!'

'All right, I won't,' said Pamela with a sigh. 'But I can't vouch for Ken! If he wants to invite Craig aboard there's nothing I can do to stop him. He's the skipper, and on this ship his word is law, as you might have noticed.'

'Yes, I had. Do you always do what he tells you?' Samantha teased.

'Only when we're sailing,' replied Pam. 'On land it's a whole different story,' she added with a grin. 'Coffee is ready, so give them a shout to come and have something to eat.'

Half an hour later, all sails set and pulling and the red ensign at its stern fluttering in the light morning breeze, *Sylphide* left the anchorage before

Craig had returned to *Blue Falcon*, much to Samantha's relief. It was another blue and gold day and once the yacht was clear of the inlet they could see in the near distance the distinctive green hills of the Dutch-French island of St Martin etched clearly against the blue sky.

The perfect weather conditions, the ideal situation being on a comfortable yacht floating gently over blue water under a sunlit blue sky with nothing to do but sunbathe and sip cool refreshing drinks, should have produced tranquillity of mind, thought Samantha, as she sat in the cockpit while John steered. But they hadn't. At least not for her. She was all on edge again, looking back all the time to see if they were being followed by a big blue ketch.

They were passing some rocky islets, chunks of pinkish brown stone, one of them shaped like a recumbent lion, when she saw at last the glimmer of a white sail against the green shape of the receding island of St Barts. She stiffened and leaned forward, as if she could see better by doing so.

'Here you are.' Pamela spoke just beside her, and looking round Samantha saw that her friend was offering her the binoculars. 'You'll be able to see if it's *Blue Falcon* much better through these.'

Samantha looked up. Pamela's eyes held a glint of derision and her lips had a mocking twist. Samantha glanced at John. He wasn't bothering to hide his amusement but was grinning widely as he looked ahead of him, watching where he was steering the yacht. On the other side of the cockpit Ken was sitting, and he was also looking at her. He didn't seem to be amused at all but was looking at her as if he didn't like her.

'Thanks,' she muttered to Pamela, took the binoculars and leaving her seat stepped up on to the after-coaming of the cockpit where she would have a better view of what was coming behind them. No doubt it was amusing to Pam and John, Craig's following them from island to island, but it wasn't funny to her. She felt as if she was being stalked by a hunter, and soon, when they reached Pinel's, she would be driven into a corner from which there would be no escape. She would be trapped and forced to face her enemy.

With the binoculars held to her eyes she scanned the wind-ruffled moving water. There was more than one yacht sailing that morning, leaving the shelter of St Barts, but at last her gaze fixed on one of the white sails. Enlarged several times by the powerful lens of the binoculars, the sail shimmered with pale yellow light as it swayed and billowed, pulling a dark blue hull through the water. Craig was following her, and there wasn't anything she could do to avoid meeting him again, so it seemed.

Returning to the cockpit, she put the binoculars back in their case. Only John was there, still steering, Pamela had gone below and Ken had gone up on the foredeck. He was, in fact, standing out on the bowsprit, leaning back against the protective railings and looking up at the sails. After a few moment's hesitation while she considered what she would say to him, Samantha stepped out on to the side-deck and walked along to the bow to lean against the lifelines and look down at the sparkling bow-wave.

'After we've been to Pinel's couldn't we go to Phillipsburg?' she asked Ken tentatively.

He looked right at her, his eyes narrow under the brim of his white-topped yachting cap.

'Why?' he asked bluntly, stepping from the bowsprit on to the deck so that he was standing beside her.

'I'd like to go to the airport near there, to catch a plane.'

'Where do you want to fly to?'

'To anywhere where I can get a flight to England. To Miami, Antigua or New York,' she replied. 'As soon as possible. Pam said you'd probably be going to Phillipsburg after visiting Anguilla, and I was wondering whether you'd mind going there today instead so ... so that I could leave.'

'My God, you've got a nerve, you know that?' he replied, his lips taut, his eyes hard. 'Asking me to change my plans just so that you can give your husband the slip! Yes, I damned well would mind going to Phillipsburg today just to suit you. And if I'd known you'd only accepted our invitation to come cruising because you wanted to run away from him I'd have never let you set foot on this yacht!'

'I ... I'm sorry,' said Samantha stiffly. 'I ... didn't know you felt like that.'

'Well, you know now,' he retorted. 'I happen to be one of the old-fashioned kind. I believe in marriage. I believe in keeping the vows I made, and I'm not going to help anyone else to split. And if your husband comes to Pinel's while we're there I'm going to ask you to leave my ship. I'm not taking you any further, neither to Anguilla or Phillipsburg. That clear?'

'Yes, it's clear,' muttered Samantha, turning away from him, her hands clenching on the wire of the lifeline, her cheeks burning suddenly. Never has she been so thoroughly put in her place or made to feel that her behaviour in running away from Craig was despicable. 'Don't worry,' she retorted rather shakily. 'Knowing how you feel now I've no wish to stay any longer on your yacht.'

'Good,' he replied shortly, and went back along the deck to the cockpit.

Alone, Samantha continued to grip the lifeline, and to stare at the foaming, hissing bow-wave, wishing she had never approached Ken and asked him to change his plans for her. After a while she heard the pad of feet coming along the hot side-deck and looking round saw Pam coming towards her.

'I'm sorry about that, Sam. It's my fault,' Pam said. 'I suppose I shouldn't have encouraged you to come with us when you told me you couldn't stay in Antigua while Craig was there. I should have realised Ken wouldn't approve.'

'Did he tell you that if Craig follows us to Pinel's Key he wants me to leave *Sylphide*?'

'Yes, he did. I tried to reason with him, but he wouldn't listen, but eventually he agreed to my suggestion that if Craig doesn't come to Pinel's he'll let you come with us to Anguilla. You can fly to the Sint Maarten airport from there.'

'Thank you,' whispered Samantha. 'I hope I haven't caused any trouble between you and Ken.'

'No more than usual,' replied Pamela with her usual cheerful grin. 'He and I don't agree on everything. He sees what you've done only from a masculine point of view. He sees you as being deceitful as well as unfaithful to the man you're married to and as far as he's concerned that's unforgivable and he doesn't want to have any part of it. But I understand why you ran away. You ran away to protect yourself from being taken over by a person who you know from past experience is capable of overwhelming you. Your instinct urged you to run away from him this time to make a point. Craig must realise that he can't dominate you all the time if he wants you back. Isn't that the message you're trying to get across to him?'

'Yes. Yes, I suppose it is,' sighed Samantha, looking over her shoulder. The blue ketch was much closer to them now, close enough to be recognisable by the device and number on its mainsail. 'I don't think I've succeeded, though, do you? He's come after me.'

'Admit, Samantha, that you'd have thought less of him if he hadn't,' remarked Pamela shrewdly. 'Admit that like most women you enjoy having a man run after you.' She laughed suddenly. 'I think the whole business is most amusing, like one of those old movies, a real romantic comedy, and I can hardly wait for the next scene to open at Pinel's Key!'

A little more than an hour later *Sylphide* was rounded up into the wind and the anchor was dropped overboard into the clear blue-green water of a wide bay sheltered from the sea by a small peninsula covered with coconut palms and sea-grape trees and edged with a wide beach of clean golden sand. Helping to furl the mainsail around the boom after it had been lowered, Samantha noticed that there were several other yachts already anchored behind the island, all of them crowded with people, presumably charter yachts, John replied in answer to her question about them.

'They're probably out for the day from Phillipsburg,' he added. 'Like to come snorkelling as soon as everything is shipshape? We might be able to catch some fish for supper.'

She agreed to go with him, thinking it would be better than just sitting around watching for *Blue Falcon* to appear in the entrance to the bay, and within a few minutes she was floating under the surface, keeping herself moving with a few lazy flicks of her flippers and watching with interest the antics of crabs scurrying sideways across the smooth sand of the bottom.

When she had tired of snorkelling she swam to the land and leaving her flippers and snorkelling mask in the shade of the trees, walked across to the other side of the narrow peninsula, to another beach. Across a narrow strip of water was the mainland of St Martin, covered with the usual thick tropical vegetation, green and hilly. There seemed to be a narrow road twisting up the hillside. A road going where? She had no idea, and wished she had thought to look at the chart of the island on *Sylphide* to see if there was a road going to a town, a centre where she could get transport to the International Airport near Phillipsburg.

With a sigh she sank down on the beach and lay back, supporting her head on her folded arms. Even if she crossed to the mainland how would she get to the nearest town? She would probably have to walk all the way, and she had no idea how far. And then, did she really want to go? Did she really want to run away from Craig any more?

Rolling over on to her stomach, she supported her head on one fist and her elbow in the sand and began to draw letters on the soft grainy sand with the forefinger of her other hand. A name was formed. *Craig*. Groaning, she laid her head down on the sand exactly where she had written the name.

What should she do? Should she stop running? Her lips twitched into a wry smile. She didn't have much option, did she, if Ken Wallis didn't want her on his yacht any more and Craig had come to Pinel's Bay? She supposed it had been a childish action on her part to leave Antigua in a huff. Had she run away as Pamela had suggested to make a point and to test Craig, to find out if he would follow her? Well, he had followed her. But what did that prove? It didn't prove that he loved her, did it? It only proved that he refused to be beaten in a battle of wills.

She stayed on the beach for a long time, thinking, trying to decide what to do next and slowly becoming aware of a heart-felt longing to give up running away and to give in to Craig, to do whatever it was he wanted her to do, facing up to the fact that no matter what he did or said, even after two years of separation she was still in love with him and wanted to be where he was. If only something could be done about Morgana Taylor!

The shadows of the palms grew longer and blacker and she realised that the sun was setting, sliding behind the hills of St Martin. It was very quiet. No sounds of people talking and laughing as there had been before. No sounds at all except the rustle of the wind on the trees and the perpetual murmur of water. A strange fear that she had been left alone in that remote place tingled along Samantha's nerves and she sprang to her feet. The hills were dark now, the water glimmering with reflected golden and crimson light.

Hurrying, her bare feet sinking in the soft dry sand, she climbed the slope of the ridge that separated one beach from another, the soles of her feet prickled by hidden palm fronds that had fallen from the trees and the sharp edges of shells half buried in the sand. The bleached twisted trunks of sea-grapes glimmered in the fast-fading light, grotesque shapes having a nightmare quality.

At last she reached the other beach. The bay spread before her, alternating patterns of dark blue and gold water, backed by the shadowy shapes of the hills. The yachts from Phillipsburg had gone. *Sylphide* had gone. Only one boat was there, lying still and quiet to its anchor line, a dark blue yacht with gold-glinting masts. Samantha stood and stared at it, feeling excitement dance along her nerves. Craig, so skilled in hunting in the forests of his native land, was waiting, concealed on the yacht, waiting for his quarry, her, to reappear. So what happened now?

Feeling the wind wafting her sun-warmed skin and chilling it slightly she shivered and clasped her arms about her. Should she swim out to the boat or would he come for her. Remembering her flippers and mask, she returned to the shadows of the trees to search, but couldn't find them. When she went back to the beach she could see a dinghy approaching, a dark shape with a dark person rowing it.

Craig beached the dinghy, pulled in the oars and taking hold of the painter stepped ashore.

'I've been waiting for you,' he said coolly. 'Ready to come aboard now?'

'Yes,' she whispered, feeling a twinge of disappointment. Why? What had she hoped for? A

warmer, more passionate reception? But why
should he greet her with more passion when she had
resisted and rejected his embraces on the beach in
Antigua? 'When did *Sylphide* leave?' she asked,
stepping into the dinghy and sitting down on the
stern thwart.

'About an hour ago. John brought your gear to
me.' He pushed the dinghy into the water and
leapt aboard. Sitting on the bow thwart, he moved
the oarlocks to the slots nearer to him, slid the
oars into them and began to row. 'Why did you go
with the Wallises?' he asked.

'They'd invited me to cruise with them ...
before you came out to Antigua ... and I thought
I'd like to see some different islands. It seemed too
good an opportunity to pass up.'

'But you didn't intend to go back to Antigua.'

'No.'

'Why not?'

'I ... I told you, when you arrived, that I
couldn't stay while you were there,' she retorted
shakily. 'And ... and when I found out that
Morgana was there too, I had to get away. Oh,
Craig, how could you do it? How could you invite
her to come out to stay there when you knew I'd
be there? How could you be so insensitive?'

'Still jealous of her?' he queried jeeringly.

She didn't answer. To admit she was still jealous
of Morgana would be to admit she was still in love
with him, wouldn't it? And she wasn't ready to do
that. Not yet. Maybe not ever. To admit she was
jealous of Morgana would be the same as saying
she still regarded Craig as belonging to her and
only to her, and then he would accuse her of being
too possessive. So she kept quiet, looking beyond

the bulk of his shoulders at the last streaks of golden light in the sky, glimmering between strips of feathery dark grey clouds.

'I didn't invite Morgana to Antigua,' Craig went on slowly. 'No one was more surprised than I was when she turned up with Conrad at Cliff House the other night.' He paused and she saw his eyes glint frostily in his shadowed face as he looked right at her. 'Then Farley passed on your message to me,' he added, his voice rasping with irritation. 'I was pretty mad, I can tell you, when I heard you'd skipped out. I'd only flown out to Antigua to see you and to put an end to our separation . . .'

'Arrogantly assuming that I would want to end it,' she accused. 'After two whole years of silence, of never writing to me, of never keeping in touch, you assumed I'd be delighted to continue with our marriage, that I'd welcome you with open arms. Oh really . . .!' She broke off, her breast heaving with indignation.

It was his turn to be quiet and there was only the creak of oarlocks as the oars rose and fell rhythmically and the gurgle of water as the dinghy approached the blue yacht. Gently the dinghy nudged against the hull of the bigger boat. Craig caught hold of the small ladder which hung down from the rail of the yacht so as to stop the dinghy from drifting away when he had shipped the oars.

'Up you go,' he ordered softly, and Samantha obeyed—what choice did she have?—climbing up and stepping into the cockpit. He followed her, tied the dinghy astern of the yacht after he had lifted the oars out of it, and stepped back into the cockpit to stand beside her. In the soft purple dusk that was weaving about them he was very close to her and she could feel his body heat radiating out to her. Deep down inside her she felt a sudden longing to be closer to him, to have his arms go around her, to put her head against his chest, but instead of stepping closer to him, instead of reaching out and touching, she stepped back, away from him.

'If you'd like to get us something to eat I'll hoist the sails and get ready to go,' he said.

'Go where?' she demanded.

'Back to Antigua,' he replied. 'It's a long haul against the wind and an adverse current, but we should be able to do it in about twelve hours if we use both sail and engine.'

'But it's dark,' she complained, looking out at the dimpling dark blue water where phosphorescence glinted. 'Couldn't we set off in the morning?'

'We could, but the sooner I get back with you the better,' he replied enigmatically, and stepping past her reached into the panel of switches which was just inside the main hatchway and flicked a couple. Immediately lights went on in the cabin. 'You'll find the refrigerator well stocked,' he said, and turning away stepped out on to the side-deck.

'You could explain,' said Samantha, and he glanced down at her.

'About what?' he asked.

'You could explain why you want to get back to Antigua with me by tomorrow morning. Oh, it was always the same. You've never explained, and yet you've always expected me to understand why you want to do certain things and you've expected me to go along with you. You . . . you've expected too much.'

He didn't say anything at first and she thought he was going to move on to the mainmast to start hoisting the sail without replying to her indignant exclamation, but he hesitated and looked down at her again.

'Perhaps I have,' he said quietly at last. 'Expected too much from you, I mean.' He drew in a breath and then let it out in a long low sigh. 'Okay, I'll try and explain. I want you to go back with me to Antigua as soon as possible and I'd like you to stay there with me for a few days, possibly no longer than a week, but long enough to convince anyone who's interested that our separation is over and that we're not going to be divorced. Could you do that? Or am I expecting too much of you, as usual?' Bitterness rasped in his voice.

'You . . . you want me to pretend our separation is over?' Samantha whispered.

'Since you don't want it to be over, yes, I guess I do want you to *pretend* that it is,' he drawled dryly.

'I . . . I'd have to know what would be involved before I could agree,' she muttered, glancing away from him down the companionway into the cabin where she could see the teak woodwork glowing cosily in the electric light. Memories of the happy times she had enjoyed with this man in that cabin three and a half years ago swamped her suddenly, and she almost cried out against the pain they induced.

'We'd just behave as if we're married,' he replied rather vaguely. 'You know, go places together, do all the things we used to do together.'

'Like . . . like sleeping together?' She forced the

question out. 'I noticed before I left Cliff House that you'd moved into my bedroom without even asking if you could,' she added, glancing up at him.

'So that's what's bothering you,' he said softly, and his teeth glinted in the light shafting upwards from the hatchway as he grinned. 'But if we don't share a bedroom everyone will assume the separation isn't over,' he pointed out coolly. 'You must see that.'

'Yes, I suppose I do,' she muttered.

'We don't have to have sex together once we're in that bedroom and the door is closed,' he went on with devastating bluntness. 'I shan't force you to do anything you don't want to do, you can be sure of that. All I'm asking is a little of your time.'

'And afterwards?' she asked.

'You can return to London, if you want to,' Craig replied with a careless shrug. 'Anyway, think about it and let me know before we get to English Harbour. I'll get the sails up now.'

He moved away and Samantha went down into the cabin. Finding her holdall on one of the bunks, she carried it into the forward cabin, stripped off her dampish *maillot* and dressed quickly in dry underwear, a shirt and sweater and jeans, thrusting her feet into her leather sailing shoes. Returning to the main cabin, she opened the small refrigerator and took out a small packet of minced meat. Soon she was shaping the meat into burgers. In a few minutes they were cooking in the frying pan on the cooker.

By the time the meat was cooked and put between slices of French bread together with an onion relish, the engine was throbbing and *Blue Falcon* was moving through the water, the sails, empty of wind, slatting noisily. Samantha carried the food she had prepared up into the cockpit and set it down on the small table attached to the wheel pedestal where Craig was standing, the wheel sliding between his big hands as he steered the yacht out of the narrow entrance to the bay.

Going back to the cabin, Samantha made two mugs of instant coffee and returned with them to the cockpit. Then she sat down in a corner, leaning against the coachroof of the cabin and facing Craig, and biting hungrily into the sandwich she had made. Above, the stars seemed to swing in the dark blue sky as the yacht swayed from side to side. At eye level the hills of St Martin were black shapes. Lower down, beyond the rail of the yacht, the water was a moving mysterious glinting mass.

'The moon is coming up,' remarked Craig, and she turned her head to look eastwards. A little lopsided but brilliantly shining, the moon was peering through the fringes of palm trees on Pinel's Key, lighting the way for them across the sea.

It wasn't the first time she had sailed with Craig by moonlight and she felt a certain contentment in being there with him. She looked away from the moon and directly at him. He was looking at her.

'Well?' he queried, and she didn't have to ask what it was he wanted to know.

'All right,' she replied. 'I'll stay with you for a while at Cliff House.'

'Thank you,' was all he said, and then the wind filled the sails as the boat surged out of the bay and on to the open sea, and he was too busy adjusting sheets and she was too busy catching plates and mugs as the yacht heeled to leeward for any further conversation.

CHAPTER FIVE

THE wharf at English Harbour was alive with movement the next morning when Samantha and Craig stepped ashore from the dinghy. Crews off the big yachts which were moored with their sterns to the old stone walls were coming and going, fetching boxes and bags of groceries, cans of petrol or oil and loading them on to the boats or taking empty cans and bags of garbage ashore. Flags, the Red Ensign, the Stars and Stripes and the distinctive red maple leaf of Canada, fluttered idly from jackposts. Masts swayed, glinting in the sunlight as the boats rocked whenever anyone stepped aboard. White hulls sparkled with reflected light, varnished superstructures gleamed, people called to each other, bare skin sometimes golden-pink, sometimes dusky brown, sometimes opaque black, shone under the caress of the already warm sun.

After having a few words with Jonas Smith, the young brother of Jeremiah the houseman at Cliff House, who looked after *Blue Falcon* whenever the yacht was in port, Craig set off across the dockyard and Samantha followed him, past the museum, past the capstans. Four days had gone by since she had left this place intending never to return and here she was back again, brought there by the man who strode ahead of her, his white-topped yachting cap set at a jaunty angle on his head, his suntanned arms and legs glowing reddish-brown

Introducing

Harlequin Temptation™

Have you ever thought
you were in love
with one man…only
to feel attracted to another?

That's just one of the temptations you'll find facing the women in new *Harlequin Temptation* romance novels.

Sensuous...contemporary...compelling...reflecting today's love relationships!

The passionate torment of a woman torn between two loves...the siren call of a career...the magnetic advances of an impetuous employer–nothing is left unexplored in this romantic new series from Harlequin. You'll thrill to a candid new frankness as men and women seek to form lasting relationships in the face of temptations that threaten true love. Begin with your FREE copy of *First Impressions*. Mail the reply card today!

First Impressions
by Maris Soule

He was involved with her best friend

Tracy Dexter couldn't deny her attraction to her new boss. Mark Prescott looked more like a jet set playboy than a high school principal–and he acted like one, too. It wasn't right for Tracy to go out with him, not when her friend Rose had already staked a claim. It wasn't right, even though Mark's eyes were so persuasive, his kiss so probing and intense. Even though his hands scorched her body with a teasing, raging fire...and when he gently lowered her to the floor she couldn't find the words to say no.

A word of warning to our regular readers: While Harlequin books are always in good taste, you'll find more sensuous writing in new *Harlequin Temptation* than in other Harlequin romance series.

® ™ Trademarks of Harlequin Enterprises Ltd.

xclusive Harlequin home subscriber benefits!

CONVENIENCE of home delivery
NO CHARGE for postage and handling
FREE *Harlequin Romance Digest* ®
FREE BONUS books
NEW TITLES 2 months ahead of retail
A MEMBER of the largest romance
fiction book club in the world

- -

GET **FIRST IMPRESSIONS**
FREE AS YOUR INTRODUCTION
TO NEW *Harlequin Temptation* ™
ROMANCE NOVELS!

 ® No one touches the heart of a woman quite like Harlequin

YES, please send me FREE and **without obligation** my *Harlequin Temptation* romance novel, *First Impressions*. If you do not hear from me after I have examined my FREE book, please send me 4 new *Harlequin Temptation* novels each month as soon as they come off the press. I understand that I will be billed only $1.75 per book (total $7.00). There are no shipping and handling or any other hidden charges. There is no minimum number of books that I have to purchase. In fact, I may cancel this arrangement at any time. *First Impressions* is mine to keep as a free gift, even if I do not buy any additional books.   142 CIX MDAR

Name

Address   Apt. No.

City   State/Prov.   Zip/Postal Code

Signature (If under 18, parent or guardian must sign.)

Get this romance novel FREE as your introduction to new

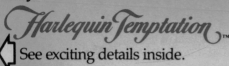

Harlequin Temptation ™

◁ See exciting details inside.

against the stark whiteness of his T-shirt and shorts.

Although he had slept only a few hours from the time the sun had come up that morning, when he had let her take over the watch-keeping from him, until she had called to him that Antigua was in sight, he didn't seem to be tired, because he walked briskly and she had difficulty in keeping up with him.

She was still a few yards behind him when he swerved to the right towards the entrance to the terrace garden of the Admiral's Inn, but he stopped short on the steps of the terrace when someone stepped out of the Inn; a woman with white-blonde hair hanging in casual ringlets about her triangular witch's face; Morgana Taylor, dressed in a sleeveless straight dress of a particularly wild shade of magenta pink scattered all over with a design of pale green leaves and pale yellow flowers, a colour which set off the pale gold tan her thin arms had acquired.

On seeing Morgana Samantha stopped too, feeling the old familiar jealousy writhe inside her, wanting to turn and run, forcing herself to stay put and pretend she didn't really care if Morgana was there or not.

'Craig darling!' Morgana gushed, going up to him her arms outstretched in greeting, putting her hands on his broad shoulders and kissing him on both cheeks, French fashion. 'When did you come back? I was so surprised when I heard that you'd gone cruising by yourself. There was no need for you to go alone, you know. I would have been delighted to keep you company.'

It was then that Morgana, on stepping back

from Craig after embracing him, saw Samantha. Her expression changed immediately. The smile with which she had greeted Craig faded and her lips tightened, and her dark eyes glittered with hostility.

'Samantha!' she exclaimed, and her voice no longer gushed with over-emphasised pleasure. She spoke almost harshly. 'What are you doing here? I thought you went away with some friends cruising through the islands. I'm sure Farley told me you wouldn't be coming back here but would be going to England when you'd finished the cruise.'

'You should never believe what young Farley says,' remarked Craig mockingly, before Samantha could think up an answer. 'What he doesn't know he makes up.' He draped an arm across Samantha's shoulder, drawing her close to him and giving her a slight hug. 'I wasn't able to leave harbour when Samantha's friends wanted to go, so she went on without me and I caught up with them. We've been cruising in company for a few days. Sam and I got back a few minutes ago and thought we'd have breakfast here on the terrace before going to Cliff House. Shall we sit over there, sweetheart?' He asked the question in a softer voice than he had used when speaking to Morgana and turned to look at Samantha when he spoke.

She nodded in agreement and he kept his arm about her shoulders as they walked over to a table in the far corner. They sat side by side on a couch. A thin brown girl with woolly black hair tied back in tight braids came to the table and took their order. As she turned to go into the inn she almost collided with Morgana, who had followed them.

'You can bring me some coffee,' Morgana said to the waitress in her most autocratic way, and sat down on a chair at the end of the table. 'Well, I must say I'm glad you're back, Craig. You're father has refused to see Dad while you've been away. Carla says he doesn't want to discuss business without you being present.' She unclasped her white leather handbag and took out a packet of cigarettes and a gold-plated lighter. 'Dad is most irritated, as you can imagine. He doesn't like to be kept waiting, even in a place as pleasant as this.'

'You didn't have to come out here with him, Morgana, you know. Your presence wasn't necessary,' drawled Craig coolly.

It seemed to Samantha that Morgana's face lost some colour took on a rather greenish tint which wasn't at all attractive and her black eyes shot sparks. The atmosphere at the table was suddenly extremely tense as Craig and Morgana stared at each other. Then Morgana laughed, arching back her long neck. Her pale hair glittered in the sunlight which was slanting down between the feathery branches of the casuarinas.

'Oh, darling, I do love you when you're being the tough hard-nosed businessman,' she said, laughter still gurgling in her throat as she leaned forward and placed a long fingered red-tipped hand over Craig's which was resting on the table. 'I'll tell Daddy what you said, but you mustn't think I've been wasting my time while I've been here. I've been having a whale of a time! I've met this most fascinating man. He's a retired navel officer and an amateur archaeologist. He's told me the most interesting stories about the island. My notebook is absolutely filled with jottings!'

Morgana's voice droned on as she talked about all she had learned of Antigua's past, and as usual she spoke only to Craig, fixing her dark eyes on his face, monopolising him completely and ignoring Samantha. Even when the waitress brought their breakfast and set the dishes of food and the coffee cups and coffee pot down Morgana didn't stop, but went on talking about the archaeological site she had been to visit the day before near the private resort of Mill Reef, the remains of an Arawak settlement.

'Brendan says radio carbon tests place the upper deposits of pottery fragments and fishbones and so on at about A.D. 1100, but the deeper layers go back another seven hundred years,' Morgana continued. 'And he says that until the Caribs got this far up the chain of islands, not long before Columbus arrived, the Arawaks lived what must have been a rather idyllic life. In fact you could say that what made a good site for a tribal settlement many years ago is also good for a modern resort community.'

Nothing had changed, Samantha thought again. It was the same as it had always been, Morgana talking and talking and talking, monopolising Craig. Oh, why had she agreed to come back here with him? She should have known it would be like this. How was she going to stand it? She glanced sideways at Craig. He had finished eating and was leaning back against the blue cushion behind him and was apparently contemplating his coffee cup while Morgana went on talking. Was he listening to her? It was hard to tell.

Suddenly, as if becoming aware that Samantha was staring at him, he slanted a glance sideways at her. His lips twitched into a slight but wickedly sardonic grin which creased his lean cheek attractively and his grey eyes glinted with amusement as he jerked his head almost imperceptibly in Morgana's direction. He closed one eye in a wink and Samantha felt a sudden uprush of affection for him. Like her, he was finding Morgana's monologue tedious and he was sharing his feeling with her. Then he turned his head and looked at Morgana and said clearly and succinctly,

'Shut up, Morgana.'

Morgana stopped talking and her mouth which was already open gaped wider, and she blinked her long mascaraed eyelashes.

'Did you say something, darling?' she asked.

'I said shut up,' replied Craig coolly. 'Samantha and I have been sailing all night and we came here hoping to have a good breakfast in peace and quiet. We don't particularly want to hear you going on and on about the plot for your next book. It sounds pretty boring to me. Do you think anyone will want to read it?'

Samantha tensed, expecting Morgana to explode in reaction to Craig's rudeness, and pretended to be engrossed pouring more coffee for herself. It seemed to take Morgana a few seconds to absorb the sense of what he had said, because there was a rather electrifying silence. Then she said with admirable smoothness,

'I do get carried away, don't I? But only when I'm with you, Craig darling.' She looked across at Samantha and smiled, her small cat-like teeth glinting. 'I'm so accustomed to telling him about everything that happens to me, you know. I've always confided in him, like a sister confides in a brother.' Her smile became a sort of grimace as her eyes grew sharp with dislike while she continued to stare at Samantha. 'Or like a wife confides in her husband,' she added provocatively.

'But you're not my sister and you're not my wife and I'm not your brother nor your husband, so you don't have to tell me about everything that happens to you and I don't have to listen,' drawled Craig, and raised a hand to signal to the waitress for the bill.

But even then Morgana didn't take the hint and go away. Turning to him, she leaned across the corner of the table and ruffled his black hair.

'Ooh, how grouchy you are this morning! I suppose you didn't have much sleep last night. All right, I'll be as quiet as a mouse and Samantha can do the talking for a change, although if my memory serves me right, she never did have much to say, and lack of conversation can be as boring as too much, I always think.' Morgana looked across at Samantha again and her brilliant smile was more like a sneer. 'Tell me,' she went on, 'have you two made it up? Have you got together again?'

'Yes, we have,' said Craig curtly.

'It would be nice, darling, if you would let your wife answer occasionally. I was speaking to her,' jibed Morgana, her lips thinning with spitefulness. 'If you get too domineering, she'll run away again, won't you, Samantha dear?' Across the table the dark eyes challenged Samantha and it took all her self-control not to spring to her feet and spit rude words of abuse at Morgana before marching away from the table. But that was exactly what Morgana wanted her to do, she realised suddenly, with a flash of insight into the woman's behaviour.

So she sat where she was and suppressing the anger which had flared up inside her returned the challenge with a bland smile while she slid her hand in the crook of Craig's arm, letting her fingers curve possessively over his warm skin.

'No, I've done with running away,' she said coolly. 'Craig and I are together again and . . . and we're going to stay that way, aren't we, Craig?' She turned towards him.

'If you say so, sweetheart,' he murmured, covering her hand with his and looking at her, and she was glad Morgana couldn't see the laughter dancing in his eyes.

'Well, all I can say is congratulations and best wishes,' said Morgana lightly, getting to her feet. 'I must rush. I promised to meet Brendan—the man I was telling you about—in the car-park at eleven-thirty and it's that time already. He's taking me to Shirley Heights and afterwards we're going to drive to St John's through the rain forest on the western side of the island. I'll tell Daddy you're back, Craig.'

'I'll have a word with him in the inn, if he's still there,' said Craig, also rising to his feet, taking the bill which the waitress had brought to him, 'I won't be long, Sam,' he added. 'I'll phone the house and ask Jeremiah to send the Caddy for us.'

Left alone at the table, Samantha watched them go towards the inn, both of them tall and having so much in common—nationality, upbringing, wealthy background, and she felt again that awful jealousy of Morgana twisting through her, in spite of Craig's rudeness to the woman. He could say as often as he liked that he wasn't Morgana's brother, but hadn't he just treated her as a brother

often treats a sister, as someone whom he found
irritating but with whom he was so close he could
speak to her frankly. And hadn't he, wasn't it
possible, that sometimes in that not too distant
past he had treated Morgana as a man might treat
his wife?

Samantha's hands clenched on her knees and
she gritted her teeth and swallowed hard.
Pretending that her separation from Craig was
over and that once more they were a loving couple
in front of Morgana hadn't been easy. Had it been
convincing? But then did Morgana have to be
convinced?

She frowned, made uneasy by the thought, and
wondered, not for the first time since Craig had
asked her to return with him to Antigua and to
stay for a while pretending that their separation
was over, why he wanted everyone to believe their
marriage had been resumed. She supposed she
should ask him why. But would he tell her?

When he eventually reappeared on the steps of
the terrace and waved to her, indicating that she
should leave the couch where she had been sitting
and join him on the steps, he was accompanied by
the tall grey-haired man who had been with
Morgana four days ago.

'I don't think you've ever met Samantha, have
you?' Craig said cheerfully, taking hold of her
hand when she reached his side. 'Sam, this is
Conrad Taylor.'

Conrad Taylor's small black eyes glittered with
enmity as Morgana's had and he didn't offer to
shake hands.

'No, we've never met,' he said shortly, 'How are
you?' he asked, barely polite, and ignoring her

murmured 'hello' he turned to Craig and said, 'I'll give some thought to what you've just told me and I'll get back to you, son.' He clapped Craig on the shoulder in what was supposedly an expression of affection and went back inside the inn.

'So that's that,' remarked Craig, tugging on Samantha's hand and swinging her round to face him. 'We came through the first and biggest test pretty well, I think. Thanks for staying cool when Morgana sneered at you. The Caddy should be waiting for us now in the car park. Come on.'

Still holding her hand, he walked away from the inn and out to the Dockyard roadway. Outside the entrance, all along the outer brick wall of the inn building cotton sun-dresses hung on hangers. Opposite to the wall on a rocky slope more dresses were displayed, together with fresh fruits and vegetables. The women who were selling sat or stood about, shouting out to anyone who was passing.

David Smith, son of Jeremiah and chauffeur and gardener to Howard Clifton, was waiting in the car park for them and soon they were driving away along the narrow road to Falmouth.

'I spoke to Carla on the phone. She's glad you've come back with me,' said Craig. 'She said my father has missed your reading to him. I took the opportunity to tell her that our separation's over and that you'll be staying as long as I will at Cliff House.'

She looked at him. His lean dark face was impassive, giving nothing away of his inner thoughts or feelings and his grey eyes, seeming paler than ever in contrast with the increased tan of his face after the last few days of sailing, regarded her steadily without a hint of mockery or any other expression.

'Why?' she demanded. 'Why do you want everyone to believe our separation is over? Is it something to do with business?'

'Maybe,' he replied evasively, and looked away from her out of the window beside him.

'John Wallis told me he'd heard that Conrad Taylor is hoping to take over Clifton's and that's why he's here in Antigua to talk with your father about it,' she said.

'Where did he hear that?'

'In the bar at the inn. Is it true?'

'Could be. Conrad is hoping to revive a discussion he had with Dad a few years ago about merging the two companies. So far he hasn't had much luck.'

'Because your father won't discuss anything with Conrad without you being present.'

'That's right.' He gave her a quick glance, his lips curving into a grin. 'You don't miss much, do you? You were listening to everything Morgana said, even though you looked half asleep.' He shifted closer to her, sitting sideways on the luxuriously thick cushioned seat, his right leg bent up. 'My father told Conrad he wouldn't discuss anything with him unless I was present, so he invited you to come here knowing I'd fly out when I knew you were here,' he added.

'I still don't understand,' she protested. 'I don't understand why you want to pretend our separation is over.'

'You don't have to understand,' he replied, leaning closer to her. 'All you have to do is be your sweet and lovely self and follow my lead, just as you have so far this morning. It shouldn't be too hard, and there'll be a few rewards for both of us along the way,' he added softly, and before she could move his lips swooped to hers, claiming them in a slow tantalising kiss.

Unexpectedly, response to the warm seductive pressure of his lips awoke abruptly. Her own lips quivered, pouted and then parted, involuntarily inviting him to continue to kiss her and to explore the warm sweetness of her mouth. But immediately his lips were still. There was a moment of motionless intensity while his lips hovered over hers, not quite touching, and then he was moving away from her.

'That's all there's time for right now, much as I would like to accept your invitation to prolong the experience,' he drawled softly. 'We'll try again later,' he added suggestively.

'Oh, I wouldn't count on it,' Samantha retorted, pretending to a coolness she wasn't feeling, pretending that her pulses weren't throbbing and that she wasn't suddenly short of breath. The car was gliding quietly down the hill towards the small sheltered bay in front of Cliff House. 'Remember you promised you wouldn't force me to do anything I don't want to do,' she said stiffly, looking away from him down at the sun-dappled water of the bay as the car swerved round the bend and into the driveway to the house.

'And you can be sure I'll keep that promise,' Craig replied smoothly, but, quiveringly aware as she was to any subtle change in him, she detected an underlying tone of irony in his voice and she looked at him sharply. His sun-hardened face looked as if it had been carved from reddish wood and was as immobile as a statue's. Only the silvery grey eyes expressed mockery. 'But I get the impression that kissing me is something you want to do not something you don't want to do,' he added outrageously.

'You're quite mistaken,' she replied, in a low voice, realising that the car had stopped, the engine had been turned off and that David probably had his ears pricked and was listening in to the conversation that was going on behind his back.

'I know I'm not,' Craig replied with a soft laugh, and his fingers lifted through the thick hair at the back of her neck in a tormenting caress.

'Please unlock the door, David,' Samantha's voice quavered with urgency as she slid to the edge of the seat, shaking off Craig's touch. 'I'd like to get out.'

'Yes, ma'am. Sorry, ma'am.' David leaned forward, flicked a switch on the dashboard and both rear doors unlocked automatically. Opening the door on her side, Samantha got out and hurried towards the house.

Carla was in the hallway waiting for them. She was smiling and she embraced Samantha warmly.

'It's good to see you again,' she exclaimed. 'Farley teased me—he told me you wouldn't be coming back here, but Craig explained and told me you'd gone away with friends and he would be meeting you and would be bringing you back.'

'Has Farley gone to Toronto?' asked Samantha, taking her holdall from Craig who had carried it into the house for her.

'Yes, he left yesterday. Will you come now to see Howard?' asked Carla. 'He said he wants to see you both as soon as you come this morning.'

'I'd like to have a bath and change before going

to see him,' Samantha replied. 'I feel all sticky with salt and I'm longing to wash my hair properly.'

'Then you do that,' said Craig crisply. 'I'll go straight to his room and you can come when you're ready. How is he today, Carla?' he asked as he and Carla turned towards the passageway leading to the east wing.

'He is well. Right now the young man is with him,' Samantha heard Carla reply as she turned away in the opposite direction to go to the west wing.

'What young man?' asked Craig.

'I forget his name. He is from the London newspaper. Didn't Howard tell you that he was expecting a journalist to come and see him? It's for the articles . . .'

Carla's voice became a mere murmur and Samantha didn't hear the rest of what the woman had to say as she moved out of earshot on her way to her suite of rooms.

To her surprise she was pleased to be back in the pleasant rooms. They were home, and after living in the confinement of a yacht for a few days it was good to have plenty of space, to be able to toss her clothing about as she stripped, to be able to walk about naked as she went from bedroom to bathroom. But best of all was the luxury of the wide bath filled to the brim with scented foam, of lying back in the warm water and relaxing, knowing that she wouldn't be disturbed for a while. Not even by Craig.

Damn! Water swirled in the bath and slopped over on to the tiled floor as she sat up suddenly, the abruptness of her movement betraying her inner irritation with herself. She began to soap herself all over, frowning all the time because she had let Craig slip into her mind. It seemed he didn't have to be in the room with her to disturb her.

What was he up to? Why did he want her to stay with him for a few days and pretend their separation was over? He hadn't told her when she had asked him in the car. He had evaded the question. *You don't have to understand*, he had said, and then he had kissed her.

Damn again. She hadn't wanted to think about that kiss either. She hadn't wanted to remember the way she had responded. It had been nothing but a reflex action on her part, she argued, as she shampooed her hair vigorously. Her lips had responded involuntarily to the touch of Craig's lips because once they had been accustomed to the feel of his lips, warm and seductive against them; because he had trained her to respond to his kiss. She hadn't really wanted to kiss him back, to invite him to prolong the kiss, to entice him to go further and explore with her the delights of sensual pleasure. Or had she?

With a sigh she lay back in the bath again. *We'll try again later*, he had said. And she knew that he would try again and would keep on trying until he had breached her fragile defences against him. Oh, he wasn't any different. He was still the man she had fallen in love with four years ago. He was still direct and forceful, overwhelming. Domineering, Morgana had called him.

Standing up, she twitched the shower curtain across and turned on the shower, letting the warm water sluice foam and shampoo away from her. *If*

*you get too domineering she'll run away again,
won't you, Samantha dear?* Morgana's cheap jibe
rang through her ears.

But Morgana had been wrong. She hadn't run
away from Craig because she had disliked his
domineering ways, Samantha thought as shining
with cleanliness she stepped out of the bath and
began to pat herself dry with a big fluffy towel.
She had run away from him because she had been
unable to share him with Morgana.

She had been happily married until Morgana
had turned up, she realised, as she watched her
reflection in the big mirror drying her hair with a
blow-dryer. Oh, damn Morgana! Why was she
always around? Why was she here in Antigua?
Why was she always coming between Craig and
herself? Why? Why?

Was she really Craig's mistress. She switched off
the dryer and leaving the bathroom went into the
bedroom and slid back the doors of the clothes
closet. There must be some way of finding out
whether Morgana and Craig were still having an
affair. Or if they had ever had an affair. Who
would know?

Carla? Samantha shook her head as she selected
a sun-dress made from crisp green cotton and laid
it on the bed. No, she doubted if the kind-hearted,
motherly Carla would know much about Morgana,
because the relationship between Craig and his
father's second wife wasn't close. Craig had never
regarded Carla as a substitute mother. When
Howard Clifton had married Carla Craig had
already been at boarding school somewhere in
Ontario and during the school holidays he had
often spent more time with his own mother in

England than he had had ever spent with Carla. So Carla was hardly likely to know much about his friendship with Morgana.

She put on clean underwear, slid the green dress on and tied the belt at her waist. Then she began to make up her face. The colour of the dress set off her tan and accentuated the green glint of her eyes. She could never compete with Morgana's dramatic appearance, but she wasn't bad-looking. Her complexion was good, her waving hair was thick and glossy and her eyes were clear.

Craig had always seemed to like the way she looked. He had *seemed* to. Her lips slipped sideways in a wry grimace. That was the trouble. He *seemed* to. She didn't actually know if he did because he had never told her. He had *seemed* to be in love with her when he had asked her to marry him, but she didn't actually know because he hadn't told her. He had seemed to think that making love to her had been enough.

Yet if he he had been away at an all-boys' school most of his childhood and youth and had been in England so much how could he and Morgana have been close? Strange that she had never thought of that before. Of course the person she should ask about his friendship with Morgana was Craig himself. But she had tried that and his replies had always been tormentingly evasive or coolly indifferent. Or he had teased her about being jealous and possessive.

She left the room and walked to the hallway. Wind was wafting through, making the leaves of the potted plants rustle, and the small yellow birds were swooping about chirping noisily.

'You see how the birds are behaving crazily,'

said Carla as she appeared from the other passageway. 'Later I think we will have a storm. The air is humid. It is, how you say, sultry? And there are clouds rolling in from the ocean. I think I will go and have a *siesta*. Howard too should have a rest, so please do not let Craig and the journalist keeping him talking much longer.'

'I'll do what I can,' said Samantha.

When she reached the door of Howard's suite of rooms she knocked. There was no answer, so she opened the door and stepped inside the spacious room. Being on the east side of the house it was in the shade most of the day, but that day, even there, the air was hot and humid.

There was no one in the room, so she went across it and stepped out on to the patio which was built on the side of the room away from the swimming pool. Howard was lying on a cushioned lounger, dressed in blue cotton trousers and a white cotton open-necked shirt. A straw hat was tilted on his head, shading his sharp hazel-grey eyes.

'It's nice to see you back, Samantha,' he said, a faint smile creasing his tanned, wrinkled face.

'It's nice to be back.' She smiled at him and put a hand in his offered one, realising with a sense of surprise that she was sincere. She was glad to be back and to see him again. Giving in to a rush of affection for him, she leaned down and kissed his cheek. 'How are you feeling today?'

'Much better for the sight of you and Craig here together,' he said softly, squeezing her hand. 'Mr Barry, this is my daughter-in-law, Samantha. I'd like you to meet Lyndon Barry from the *News Chronicle*, Clifton Enterprises' British daily.'

Lyndon! Samantha felt sweat break out on her skin. Her head seemed to spin. Lyndon here? She managed to control the start of surprise and turned to look at the young man, with untidy brown hair topping a long thin face adorned with a shaggy brown moustache, who was sitting on a deck chair beside a round patio table and who was staring at her incredulously.

'Samantha!' he exclaimed, jumping to his feet and knocking something off the table which fell with a clatter on the stone flags of the patio. 'What are you doing here?'

'You two know each other?' Craig spoke sharply. Arms folded across his chest, he was sitting in another deck chair on the other side of the table from Lyndon.

'We certainly do,' said Lyndon. He was still staring at her as if he couldn't believe his eyes. Samantha forced herself to smile at him while wishing he would vanish into thin air.

'Hello, Lyn,' she said. 'This is a surprise, isn't it? As you know,' she continued, turning to Craig, who was watching Lyndon with slitted assessing eyes, '*Woman's Insight* and *News Chronicle* are housed in the same office block, so of course Lyn and I have met several times.'

'I see,' drawled Craig, flicking her an icy look.

'But I didn't know that she ... I mean that Samantha is your wife,' explained Lyndon. 'I ... knew she's married, but. . . .' he broke off, looking confused, and gave Samantha a puzzled, rather hurt glance.

'I've always used my family name at work,' Samantha said quickly, 'so naturally Lyndon didn't know my married name of Clifton.'

'Naturally,' drawled Craig dryly, and she flashed him a wary glance. His lips were curling in a sardonic expression. 'Have you finished interviewing my father, Barry?'

'Er—yes, for today, that is,' replied Lyndon, picking up the small microphone which he had knocked to the ground when he had stood up and then collecting the tape recorder to which it belonged from the table. 'But I would like to come back tomorrow, if I may, sir, for photographs.'

'Tomorrow morning at ten sharp,' replied Howard. 'If you're any later you'll have to manage with any photographs of me your newspaper has in its files—and it should have a good selection, since I own it.'

'I'll be here, sir, at ten,' said Lyndon. 'Would it be possible for me to call a taxi now?' he added hopefully. He was looking a little flustered and sweat was shining on his skin.

'Where are you staying?' asked Craig, rising to his feet.

'At the Lagoon Hotel. It's just down the road.'

'I'll drive you there,' said Craig crisply. 'Come on.'

'Er—thanks,' muttered Lyndon. 'I'll see you tomorrow, then, sir,' he said to Howard as he passed him. 'You too, Samantha?' He gave her a quick appealing glance and then followed Craig into the house.

'Sit down, Samantha,' Howard requested gently. 'No need for you to go yet. Tell me, why didn't you ever tell that young man you were married to a Clifton?'

Sitting down on the chair that Lyndon had recently vacated, Samantha pushed her heavy hair back from her face and lifted it up from the back of her neck. The humid heat was getting to her. Even though the wind was blowing all the time it brought no relief today. The atmosphere was growing more and more oppressive.

'I . . . I . . . don't know. It just never occurred to me to tell him,' she explained. She looked up at him. 'We didn't talk much about ourselves,' she added.

'He never asked you about your husband, where he lived or why you were separated from him?'

'Yes, he did, and I told him the truth, but I didn't mention Craig's name.' She paused and frowned with the effort of explaining. 'I think I didn't tell Lyn or anyone else who worked in the London offices of Clifton Enterprises that I was related to you by marriage in case it was thought I'd got my job through yours or Craig's influence,' she added slowly.

'Mmm. That was wise of you,' Howard said approvingly, and there was a short silence. 'But if you never talked about your relationship with Craig to Mr Barry, where did he get the information that you're planning to divorce Craig?'

Samantha looked up sharply at the dark eagle-beaked face. The hooded yellowish-grey eyes were watching her closely.

'I . . . I did mention to Lyn once that I'd been to see a lawyer to get advice about a divorce,' she whispered truthfully.

'And you're quite sure you didn't tell him the name of your husband then?'

'Quite sure.' She returned his penetrating gaze steadily.

'I believe you,' he said with a sigh. 'Then where the hell did he hear such a rumour?'

'I don't know. Oh, surely he didn't ask you about it?' she exclaimed, dismayed that Lyndon should stoop to asking a question that was based on gossip or rumour.

'He had the effrontery to ask me if there was any truth in the rumour that's going about this part of Antigua, among the millionaire set, he said, that the wife of my eldest son is about to sue him for divorce,' replied Howard flatly, his lips curving cynically. 'And consequently he made me damned sorry I'd agreed to let him come out here from London to interview me. For years I've avoided being interviewed by the media, knowing what little respect for a person's private life a lot of those interviewers have and how they'll distort the truth. But this was a special occasion; the occasion of my retirement from the chairmanship of Clifton's, so I agreed to let all the newspapers I've owned publish an article about me. But damn it all,' he struck the arm of the lounger with his clenched fist, 'I'd hoped that a journalist from one of my own newspapers would be more tactful and steer clear of personal questions!' He leaned back against the cushions of the lounger and closed his eyes, looking suddenly very tired and frail.

'Was Craig here when Lyn asked the question?' asked Samantha, and he opened his eyes to look at her again.

'No, he wasn't, thank God.' His eyes narrowed. 'Are you still planning to divorce Craig? I thought ... at least I'd been told by Carla this morning, that you and he have decided to end your separation.'

'Yes, we have,' she replied, remembering the pretence she was supposed to be keeping up.

'I'd glad to hear it. I wouldn't like you to do to him what his mother did to me,' said Howard, and the bitterness in his voice shocked her.

'What did she do to you?' she whispered, thinking of the beautiful Ashley who hadn't understood him, had found him too deep and too silent.

'She married me for my money and as soon as she could she divorced me for money too,' he said dryly. 'It happens all the time, but I'm not going to stand by and let it happen to Craig. Do you hear?' He glared at her fiercely. 'There's no way he's going to be divorced by you on some trumped-up accusation of cruelty or anything else so that you can rook him for a million-dollar settlement. If there is going to be a divorce *he'll* divorce you!'

'There . . . there isn't going to be a divorce,' she said rather shakily.

'That's what I told Mr Barry. And I told him to be sure to scotch the rumour any way he can. But I wish I could find out who started the rumour.' He gave her another sharp glance. 'You might try to find out, Samantha.'

'Yes, I will,' she promised.

'I feel very tired now,' he muttered, 'And there's a storm brewing. I guess we'll all feel edgy and bad-tempered until it breaks, so if you don't want to quarrel with Craig stay away from him until it's over,' he added with a fleeting grin that gave him a brief resemblance to Craig. 'You might tell Jeremiah to come to me, now.'

He closed his eyes again and Samantha stood up. She would have liked to have asked him if he had any suspicions about who would spread the rumour he had told her about, but he looked so pale and exhausted that she decided it was better not to.

'I'll go and tell Jeremiah,' she told him, touching his shoulder as she passed him on her way into the house.

She met Jeremiah in the passageway.

'Mr Craig phoned, ma'am,' he said politely. 'He left a message to say he's gone to St John's and will be back later.'

'Thank you, Mr Clifton asked me to tell you to go to him now. He's feeling very tired,' said Samantha. 'If Mr Craig or anyone else should phone, I'll be in my room, Jeremiah.'

'Yes, ma'am.'

CHAPTER SIX

SAMANTHA lay on the bed in her room and stared through the patio window at the play of sunlight and shadow on the concrete surround of the swimming pool. The window was closed and the air-conditioning unit was on, whirring quietly, cooling the room.

Why had Craig gone to St John's? Had he gone to meet Morgana? Had he made an arrangement to meet Morgana in the capital when he had walked with the woman into the Admiral's Inn? Had that little scene that had been performed in the terrace garden been just that—a performance, put on by Craig and Morgana to deceive her into thinking that they were not the close friends she had always believed them to be? Had Craig's rudeness to Morgana been nothing more than a deliberate pretence to blind his wife to the truth?

She shifted restlessly on the bed, wishing she could turn off her imagination as she might have turned off a TV set, and reminded herself that her separation from Craig wasn't really over. She had no right to be wondering where he was just because he wasn't with her. He didn't have to be with her all the time and she didn't have to be with him all the time. Closing her eyes, she drifted off to sleep and didn't waken until she heard someone knocking on the bedroom door.

It was Jeremiah, to tell her that a Mr Barry wished to speak to her on the phone and that she could take the call on the extension in her sitting room.

'Thank you.' Still dazed with sleep, she looked at her watch and saw with surprise that it was quarter to five. She had slept more than two hours. 'Has Mr Craig come back from St John's yet?' she asked as she followed Jeremiah into the sitting room.

'No, ma'am, not yet,' he replied, and left the room.

Samantha curled up in a corner of the couch and picked up the receiver of the red telephone which was on a teak coffee table.

'Hello, Lyn. I'm glad you've called,' she said. 'I owe you an apology.'

'You most certainly do,' he replied. 'But we can't talk about it over the phone. Could you come to the hotel? We could have a drink and dinner together and you could explain.'

'I'll be there in a half an hour,' she replied.

'I'll be waiting for you at the entrance.'

She replaced the receiver and getting to her feet stretched her arms above her head. The sleep, for all that it had been haunted by dreams about Craig and Morgana, had done her good, and going to see Lyn to try and explain to him why she had never told him she was married to Craig Clifton would be better than staying in the house wondering where Craig was.

In the bedroom she changed into another sun-dress, made from beautifully screen printed local cotton, a pattern of dark blue leaves on a background of turquoise that she had bought in a fashion boutique in St John's. Leaving her shoulders completely bare, the shirred bodice of the dress was held up by a frill of material that went right round the bodice top and across her arms. The skirt was full, falling from gathers, and was belted at the waist.

When she was ready David drove her to the hotel in a Hustler, a small jeep-like vehicle with no doors, manufactured on the island from parts imported from other countries. Since it had no doors it was ideally air-conditioned. Dust or rain could be kept out by unrolling plastic screens which were tied up to the roof.

The sun was still shining, but the sky had a leaden quality and the palm trees lining the approach to the hotel were unusually still. For once the wind wasn't blowing. The stillness, the yellow tinge in the sky, the humid heaviness of the air created an uneasy atmosphere; a suspenseful calm before a storm.

In the wide foyer of the hotel, a place of dim coolness, Lyn was waiting for her. He was dressed in pale beige slacks and a matching shirt. There was a certain coolness in the way he greeted her and he didn't smile.

They sat at a table in a courtyard between the main building of the hotel and the big swimming pool. Many of the guests were either sitting at tables or standing around talking and drinking. Waiters and waitresses from the bar in the hotel moved about with trays laden with drinks. In one part of the courtyard some young men all dressed alike in white cotton slacks and bright wildly patterned cotton shirts were rolling steel barrels into position.

'It's a well-known steel band,' Lyn explained to Samantha. 'Today is Shrove Tuesday and the management here has laid on a festival dinner-dance. Dinner is a barbecue buffet, served out here by the pool. You'll stay?'

'If you'd like me to.' She sipped some of the Planter's Punch he had ordered for her. 'Lyn, it is just a coincidence that you were sent here to do that interview with Howard Clifton, isn't it? I mean, you really didn't know I was here.'

'I really didn't know you were here. In fact I didn't know you'd left *Woman's Insight* until a few days ago when I called in the editorial offices to see you and to tell you I'd got this assignment. No one there seemed to know where you'd gone, so I phoned your flat.' Lyn laughed shortly. 'Thea, your flatmate, was very offhand and said she hadn't the slightest idea of where you were or when you'd be coming back. She refused to give me your parents' home address too, but I remembered you'd once told me they lived in Epping. Then I was stumped because I didn't know their last name.' His lips twisted wryly. 'At least, I thought I didn't. I'd always assumed that Lewis was the name of your husband, for some reason. Stupid of me, I admit, in this day and age when so many women don't change their last name when they marry.' He gave her a bitter glance over the top of his glass as he raised it to his lips. 'But you did,' he accused.

'Yes, I did. Lyn, I had reasons for not using the name Clifton. I didn't want anyone to think that I'd got my job just because I was married to Craig. I . . . well, I don't much care for nepotism.'

'I can understand that,' he said. 'But what I can't understand is why you couldn't have told me who your husband is. I thought we were friends. I wouldn't have betrayed your confidence. I wouldn't have told anyone on the magazine staff or on the *Chronicle*'s staff.'

'I couldn't be sure of that,' she explained. 'I'm sorry if I hurt your feelings.'

'I'm more disappointed than hurt,' he replied. 'I like you, Sam, and I was beginning to think that perhaps you and I could be more than just friends. Especially when you told me that you'd been to see a lawyer about getting a divorce.' He gave her a curious underbrowed glance. 'But I know now that you won't be going any further with that. Old man Clifton was very emphatic about it. No chance of you divorcing his son and rooking him for a cool three-million settlement like Ashley Colter did. "*There will be no divorce*," he said, just like that, as if his word was law, and then he gave me a lecture on not liking interviewers who asked personal questions. All I did was ask him if the rumour I had heard was true.'

'I know. He told me,' said Samantha, looking up at the sky. It was covered now by low grey nimbus clouds and they had almost covered the sun, yet the atmosphere was still hot and humid. 'Did you feel rain?' she asked.

'No. But it looks as if it might pour at any minute. I see they're beginning to serve the food. Let's go and join the queue and get a table under the shelter on the other side of the pool,' Lyn suggested, rising to his feet.

But they never reached the group of hotel guests who were already serving themselves at the long tables where stainless steel dishes kept hot by gas flames underneath them were set out, full of appetising food; barbecued chicken and spare ribs, thick chunks of ham with pineapple rings, spicy beef stew, mounds of rice, and fresh bread rolls. Before they could even pick up a plate the storm broke violently and noisily. Wind swished through the trees and shrubs. Sheets of rain, each drop seeming as hard as a hailstone, swept across the courtyard, driving everyone under the narrow shelter where actually there was no shelter because the wind flung the rain in under the roof, soaking all the people who had sheltered there. Lightning crackled and flickered, livid streaks of light, and thunder banged and rolled.

'Not much point in staying out here,' said Lyn, who had managed to pile two plates full of food. 'Let's run with the rest for shelter.'

With others who had the same idea they raced across the courtyard, plates in hand, dodging among the members of the steel band who, without having played a note of music, were trying to get to shelter too, lugging their steel barrels. Everyone made for the lounge bar, a big room with tables and chairs. The manager appeared, to apologise for the weather and to announce that the food would be brought in and set out in the breakfast room nearby, that the band would be playing in the dance area in the dining room and that the guests wouldn't be charged for dinner that night. Dinner was on the house and the Mardi-Gras festival evening would continue. Cheers and applause greeted his last statement.

There was no chance of Samantha and Lyn discussing anything of a private and personal nature while they ate, because they were joined at a table in the breakfast room by another couple, also from England, who were on their honeymoon.

Not until the meal was over and they left the breakfast room to wander through to the foyer, which was quiet and deserted, everyone having crowded into the dining room to listen and dance to the rhythms of the steel band, was conversation without shouting possible.

'You said that you'd heard a rumour that Craig was going to be divorced,' said Samantha. 'Where? Since you came to Antigua?'

'That's right. On my first night here, two nights ago. I went down with some of the guests from here to the Admiral's Inn—got talking to some Canadians who were staying there and told them why I was here. They seemed to know the Clifton family quite well and one of them mentioned that Craig Clifton's wife had been seeking a divorce.'

'A woman? Was it a woman who told you the rumour?'

'Yes. Does it matter?'

'What did she look like?' persisted Samantha. 'Was she tall and did she have lots of blonde ringlets?'

'Yes, she did. You know her?' Lyn's eyes narrowed.

'Morgana. Morgana Taylor,' muttered Samantha. 'Oh, I should have guessed! She's done nothing but cause trouble between me and Craig.'

'In what way?'

'They've known each other for years and at one time there was talk of them getting married to each other. But Craig married me instead and she's always resented the fact,' said Samantha, her voice low and edged with bitterness. 'Whenever she's around and he and I are together she monopolises him and makes me feel ... well, to tell the truth, Lyn, she makes me feel as if I'm the outsider.'

'She makes you feel as if you're the gooseberry and he and she are the lovers and that they would be very glad if you'd get lost,' Lyn suggested dryly.

'That's it. That's just how I feel when she's with us. And it makes me . . . it makes me want to run away,' she muttered.

'And now she's spreading rumours about you,' he remarked. 'But you must know, Samantha, that a rumour is usually spread by someone who's in the dark and is trying to find out the truth of a situation. We journalists do it all the time,' he went on with a grin. 'I suspect this Morgana Taylor would like you to divorce Craig, or him to divorce you. But she doesn't know or isn't sure of how things are between you and him.' He frowned and his mouth twisted as he looked beyond her at the rainswept darkness they could both see through the open front doors of the hotel. 'Neither do I know how things are between you and your husband, in spite of what old man Clifton said,' he added, and flicked a glance at her. 'You did tell me you were considering a divorce, when we were in London, you know.'

'But that was before . . .' Samantha broke off, biting her lip and avoiding his probing stare.

'Before what?' he queried. 'What's happened? Has that cold-eyed devil put some sort of pressure on you to stay married to him?'

'No. No pressure,' she said as lightly as she could. 'We just decided to end our separation, that's all.'

'To please the old man?' he suggested. 'So that everything in the Clifton family garden looks rosy to the outside world on the occasion of his retirement?'

'Oh, no, he had nothing to do with it,' said Samantha quickly, and when he continued to look unconvinced she remarked, 'You'll have to be careful, Lyn—being a newspaper reporter is beginning to get to you. You're becoming cynical.'

'Perhaps I am. It seems to have come about so quickly, the ending of your separation. Hardly a month has passed since we were having lunch together in a pub in London and you were telling me you'd been to see a lawyer to ask advice about a divorce, and now you're telling me your separation is ended. It all seems too easy, too smooth somehow not to have been deliberately arranged.' He gave her another sharp glance as he raked shaggy brown hair back from his forehead. 'How did you come to fly out here, anyway? Did your husband invite you?'

The question surprised Samantha, and she was about to answer negatively and tell him that Howard Clifton had invited her when she saw very clearly what Lyn would deduce from such information. He would infer that because her father-in-law had invited her to come to Antigua and then Craig had turned up Howard had manipulated an end to their separation; that it had been ended (at least for a few days) to please the 'old man' and make everything in the Clifton garden look rosy.

'I was invited, yes,' she replied vaguely, and looked at her watch. It was almost nine o'clock. Would Craig be back at Cliff House yet? 'I must be getting back,' she muttered.

'Does Craig know you came here to see me?' Lyndon asked.

'No. He'd gone out, to St John's, but he should be back by now.' She stood up. 'I'll take a cab from the front—there're usually a few waiting for customers. I'll probably see you again tomorrow when you come to take the photographs. I'll ask Carla to invite you to stay to lunch afterwards.'

'No photographs and no lunch,' he said wryly.

'Oh. Why not?'

'I was warned off by your husband, when he drove me back to the hotel. He told me to make do with the photographs in the *Chronicle*'s files and that he didn't want me to return to Cliff House.' He laughed a little. 'And since he's bigger than me in more ways than one I didn't argue! He could lose me my job. I fly back to London tomorrow afternoon.' They had reached the front doors. 'Look, Sam, why don't you come back with me? I'm sure they'd be glad to see you again at *Woman's Insight*.'

'But I don't have a job there any more,' she replied. 'You must know that orders were received from on high to reduce the editorial staff. I was the one who was cut.'

Lyn stared at her incredulously.

'You were sacked?' he exclaimed. 'I was told you'd resigned.'

'No. I was the victim of an economy drive.'

'What economy drive? There was no cut-back of staff of the magazine.'

'But Marilyn Dowell, the managing editor, assured me there was. She said the orders had come directly from. . . .' Samantha paused, her eyes widening as she realised for the first time the real meaning of what she was going to say. 'Marilyn said she'd been told directly by top brass to cut back on her staff,' she added weakly.

'And you've only just realised who that top brass is, haven't you,' said Lyn dryly. 'Samantha, you've been manipulated and duped by a very cunning old man. Or possibly by his son. So why stay with them? Come back with me to the U.K. tomorrow.'

'No, I can't. I must go now. Goodbye, Lyn— nice seeing you again.'

She sped down the shallow flight of steps to one of the waiting taxis and was soon being driven back to Cliff House. The rain had stopped and the sky was clearing rapidly, clouds being rolled back by the wind which had come back. As the taxi lurched down the hill towards the bay in front of Cliff House she saw the moon coming up above the dark horizon; a round disc shining with soft golden radiance.

In front of the house the Cadillac glinted in the light slanting out from the windows, and after paying and tipping the taxi driver Samantha ran into the hallway. Jeremiah appeared as if by magic.

'Do you know where Mr Craig is?' she demanded.

'He said he was going to walk along the beach, ma'am, and maybe he'd go swimming. I warned him it might not be safe. That storm has sure churned up the water and . . .'

Samantha didn't stay to hear what else Jeremiah had to say. Dumping her handbag on a convenient couch, she ran from the hallway and down the steps again, past the Cadillac and along the path to the cliffside steps. Electric lights set into the rocks at intervals illuminated the steps and she had no difficulty in seeing her way down to the beach, but once she was on the soft sand she became confused by the moving shadows of the palms that were swaying in the light night breeze and was unable to see whether Craig was walking along the beach or not.

Surf edging the waves which were pounding against the shore, driven in by the wind, glittered with light reflected from the steps as well as from the moon which was now sailing the sky. Going to the edge of the surf, Samantha peered out at the dark heaving mass of water, searching for the shape of a head, for the flash of phosphorescence as someone's arm lifted above the surface in a crawl stroke. But she could see nothing. Slowly she began to wander along the sand, always looking about her, trying to pierce the shadows, looking for Craig, and gradually the anger in her began to fade, its place taken by anxiety. Supposing he had gone swimming and had got into difficulties and drowned . . .?

When she reached the end of the beach she stopped walking, not wanting to climb over rocks in the dark. Turning, she began to hurry back the way she had come, wondering whether to shout Craig's name and deciding against it because he wouldn't be able to hear her calling above the boom and hiss of the waves, and all the time she kept looking about her, at the sea, at the tree-shadows. Even so when he did step out of the cluster of trees where the windsurfers were stored she was startled.

'Oh, I've been looking for you,' she exlaimed. 'Where've you been?'

'In the sea.'

'Jeremiah said that he warned you it wasn't safe

to swim tonight,' she rebuked him. 'And when I couldn't find you I thought . . .' She broke off to shudder. 'Oh, it doesn't bear thinking about,' she whispered.

'You were anxious?' He sounded surprised.

'Of course I was.' She dared to look at him then. His skin and hair were glittering with diamond drops of water reflecting the moonlight. 'I . . . I've always worried when you've gone off to do dangerous activities like hang-gliding and sky-diving . . .'

'Then you should have come with me and learned how to hang-glide and sky-dive too, and then you would have known what was involved. You would have learned how careful I am, how I don't take chances and obey all the rules of safety,' he replied quietly.

'How could I go with you? You never asked me to. Not once,' she retorted, then added in a lower tone, 'And after a while I began to think you didn't really want me to go anywhere with you and to wonder why you'd married me.'

It wasn't what she had intended to say to him at all. She had intended to accuse him of having had her sacked from *Woman's Insight* and to tell him that she wasn't going to pretend that their separation was over just to please his father; she had intended to tell him that she would be leaving on the next flight out of Antigua for London, and that this time she would be leaving him for ever. But her anger had been dissipated by anxiety about him and anxiety had brought to her a realisation of how much she loved him and how much she wished their separation was really at an end.

'I didn't know that,' he said softly, stepping closer to her, peering down at her moonlit face, his eyes glittering like the diamond drops of water on his skin and hair. 'You never told me how you felt, and after a while I began to think you didn't really care about me and that you'd married me—as many of my friends and relatives were fond of telling me—because I was a good catch for someone like you; that you'd married me because I was wealthy.' His voice rasped bitterly. 'Even in bed you didn't give of yourself entirely, you were always holding back, until I got the impression that you didn't want me to make love to you.' He paused to wipe away water which had dripped from his hair on to his face and then continued in a colder, harder tone. 'You're still holding back,' he accused. 'You're still refusing to give, to meet me halfway, and today I've found out why.' His breath hissed as he drew it in between his teeth and his eyes flashed angrily in the moonlight. 'You've been with Lyndon Barry this evening, haven't you?'

Inwardly shattered by the view he had of her as a woman who had married only for money, for what she could get out of him in the way of material possession and who was cold and unloving, Samantha stared at him speechlessly, wanting to protest but unable to find a way; wanting to explain to him that she had held back when he had made love to her because she had been convinced he was in love with Morgana.

'Well, haven't you?' he demanded harshly, 'Been to the hotel to see Barry?'

'Yes—yes, I have,' she stammered. 'I . . . I've been to see him. I had to explain to him why I hadn't told him I'm married to you and . . .'

'Don't bother to make excuses,' he sneered. 'I'm only surprised you've returned so early. I'd have thought you'd have stayed the night with him while you could.'

'Oh!' There was a roaring in her ears and the red mist of anger seemed to hover before her eyes, blinding her. She wanted to strike out at him, hit him for insulting her, and she did actually raise a hand. But suddenly the mist cleared away and the roaring stopped and she saw him very clearly, his skin silvered by the moonlight, a tall strong man who stood proudly erect and looked down at her directly, challengingly. This was the man she had fallen in love with four years ago; the man she had married and with whom she had enjoyed magical moments and she had just intended to strike him for implying that she had been sleeping with another man. What had happened to them? Why were they quarrelling like this? Where had they gone wrong?

'I . . . I do believe you're jealous,' she drawled, mocking him a little as he had so often mocked her when she had objected to his friendship with Morgana, and instead of hitting him she reached out and touched his chest lightly.

'You're damned right I am!' he growled, and when she would have withdrawn her hand he caught it in his and held it right where it was, against his chest while he stepped closer to her until their hands were trapped between his chest and her breasts. 'And when Jeremiah told me where you'd gone I was tempted to go to the hotel, punch Lyndon Barry on the jaw and drag you away from him!'

'So now you know how I feel and always have

felt when I know you've been with Morgana,' Samantha whispered shakily.

'But you've had no reason to be jealous of her,' he replied. 'No reason at all.'

'Oh, yes, I have,' she retorted, stepping away from him, trying to pull her hand free of his and failing. 'Whenever I'm with you and she turns up she monopolises you and makes sure I feel unwanted. And ... and for all I know, you and she have been carrying on an affair for years. For all I know you and she could have been living together for the past two years.'

'So?' Craig's hand tightened painfully on hers and he jerked her roughly towards him so that she fell against his chest. She tried to push away from him, her free hand flat against him, but he dropped her other hand and put both arms around her, to hold her closely. His face close to hers, he spoke softly and succinctly into her right ear, his breath feathering the delicate skin, sending tiny shivers of sensuousness along delicate nerves. 'For all I know you've been carrying on an affair with Lyndon Barry for the past two years and living with him. He could be the reason why you've been getting advice from a lawyer about divorcing me.'

'But ... how ... who told you I've been to see a lawyer?' she gasped.

'Never mind how I know. I do,' he replied dryly. 'Going to deny it?'

'No,' she whispered. Strange things were happening to her legs. They were beginning to shake and she was having to lean against him. Through the thin cotton of her dress she could feel the muscles of his thighs flex as he took her weight and supported her. Under the palm of her hand which was still laid flat against his chest his skin was warm and still damp from the sea, enticing her fingers to stroke it intimately. Being close to him was arousing that deep dark urgency within her. She could feel it uncoiling within her and spreading through her loins. Desperately she pushed against his chest again. 'Let me go,' she whispered. 'Oh, please let me go!'

'No, not now. Not until I've had what I want from you,' Craig murmured thickly, and his hands began to move over her back suggestively, pressing her more closely against him, and she could feel his fingers searching for and finding the zip which fastened the low-cut bodice of her sun-dress at the back.

'But you promised you wouldn't,' she protested, but her heart wasn't in the protest and she made no further attempt to push him away. She couldn't, because desire was licking along her veins like red flames and she wanted nothing more than to give in to the wild wantonness that was sweeping through her. 'Please!' she pleaded huskily, lifting her head to look up at him, her lips parting, her eyelids dropping as she unwittingly tempted him to kiss her, although she had really meant to ask him again to let her go.

'Please what?' he mocked softly. 'Please do this, do you mean?' And his lips brushed across hers provocatively, leaving them to ravage her throat, while he stroked the frill of material that held her dress down her arms. Unbelted now, the dress slid down slowly to lie in a pool of moonlit turquoise at her feet. 'I promised only not to do anything you didn't want to do,' he whispered softly, then his voice cracked and he added roughly as he surveyed her moonlit bare body, 'I want you, Samantha.'

At his touch her breasts seemed to unfurl like a rosebud unfurls to the caress of the sun, and within her the dark flame of desire blazed up, consuming the frail defences she had built against it. Her arms went around him, her fingernails dug into the smoothness of his shoulders and her lips lifted to his in hungry demand.

Seemingly melded together by the heat of their separate passions, they rocked for a while on their feet, then moving as one sank down to lie on the sand, closely entwined. Moonbeams slanting through the fringed fronds of the palms danced on their bare skins and struck sparks from their eyes. A few yards away the surf whispered and hissed. Above them the palm-fronds swayed and rustled in the night wind. Beneath them, the soft sand, untouched by the sea and sheltered from the rain during the storm, was still warm. It shaped into a couch, lapping their bodies.

Craig caressed her with a sort of suppressed violence as if he was having difficulty in holding in check an overwhelming desire to take her. But she was more than ready to respond, and there was violence too in the way she touched him. The need to possess and be possessed was a temporary insanity, a delicious all-consuming fury, so that they both pinched and scratched, licked and bit in their desperate attempts to convey their feelings, and their union was a sudden shocking explosion of sensation.

Sobbing with relief, tears scalding her cheeks, Samantha lay curled up against him and slowly a sweet aftermath flowed through her body, an easing of tension such as she had never experienced before. She felt she could have stayed there for ever with her head pillowed by his warm pulsing body, feeling his fingers lifting lazily through her hair, hearing the night wind sighing through the trees and the surf whispering to the sand.

So often she had felt like this after they had made love in the early days of their marriage, Samantha thought hazily, before Morgana had come on the scene and had had the effect of freezing her responses to his kisses and his touch, had caused her to hold back from loving him.

No, it had never been this good. She had never felt so replete before as if every craving had been completely satisfied. But why did she feel this way? Because she had given of herself recklessly, without fear of the consequences, because she hadn't been able to control the surge of passion which had swept through her knocking aside all barriers. For a few moments she had experienced a great freedom of body and soul, as if Craig's lovemaking had released her from a prison to which she had condemned herself to live in ever since she had separated from him.

But they were still separated. They were only together because they were pretending not to be separated for a few days, possibly a week, he had said, and then she could go back to London if she wanted. He didn't love her as she wanted to be loved. He would have asked her to stay with him for ever, if he did, and just now he had used her, treated her not as the woman he loved but as a sex object. All the lovely langourous contentment drained out of her in a revulsion of feeling, and pushing away from him she sat up. Immediately

Craig jack-knifed into a sitting position beside her. His bare arm brushed against hers and she shuddered, cringing away from him, afraid her senses might be overwhelmed again by the attractions of his sleek sun-tanned, sea-scented skin, his hard sinewy thighs, the magic in his fingertips.

'What's wrong?' he whispered.

'You took advantage of the situation,' Samantha groaned. 'Oh, now what am I going to do?'

'I only took what's mine,' he replied with a touch of arrogance, and slid a hand suggestively along her thigh. 'I gave something too,' he added provocatively, his head tilting down towards hers, his smiling lips within an inch of hers. 'And you didn't seem to mind. You took and gave back more freely than I've ever known you do. It was good, very good, and there's more if you want it, but not here. In bed, and afterwards—we can sleep together.'

'No, no!' She flung herself sideways, rolling away from him, from the exquisite temptation of his touch, and sprang to her feet. 'I can't bear it,' she muttered to herself frantically. 'I can't bear for you to touch me!'

Seeing her dress still lying where it had dropped, she snatched it up and stepped into it, pulling it up over her nakedness, her fingers groping for the zip at the back.

'Samantha, sweetheart!' Craig was on his feet and coming towards her.

'No!' Picking up her sandals, she turned and dashed over the heaps of sand to the steps.

'Samantha, come back!' Craig shouted after her, but she didn't stop. She was determined to escape from him again, afraid of the power he could exert over her. Up the steps she ran, along the path, into the house and along the dimly lit passage to her rooms. Once in the bedroom she went straight to the clothes closet and slid back the doors. She yanked out her suitcases and began to pull her clothes off the hangers, her breath coming out in panting sobs.

'What the hell are you doing?' Craig burst into the room and slammed the door behind him. He had been running too and he stood still for a moment in front of the door, his hands on his hips just above the place where his blue bikini swimming briefs curved against his tanned skin, and his chest was rising and falling as he too gasped for breath. Under frowning eyebrows his light eyes glittered angrily.

'Can't you see?' Samantha retorted, bundling the clothes she had taken from the hangers into one of the suitcases. 'I'm packing. I'm leaving!'

'Now?' he queried, and began to walk slowly across the room towards the bed where she had lifted the case to pack it.

'Now,' she repeated. 'I . . . can't do what you asked me to do. I can't stay and . . . and pretend we're not separated . . . not if you're going to take advantage of the situation and make . . . make love to me. I . . . I refuse to be treated as a plaything!'

'And where will you run to at this time of night?' he drawled. 'To the hotel? To spend the night with Barry? Over my dead body! You're not his—you're mine.'

'I . . . I'm not!' she flared, making the mistake of looking up from what she was doing and looking at him, feeling her legs turn to water at the sight of him, reddish-brown skin glowing in the lamplight, wide shoulders and broad chest curving in to a lean waist and hips.

'Oh, yes, you are,' he added softly, advancing upon her his feet sinking into the deep pile of the carpet, his eyes narrow, glinting between dark lashes as their glance lingered on her face. 'You still wear my ring and you're still my wife in the eyes of the law. That hasn't changed, and it isn't going to change unless *I* decide to change it. You're not going anywhere tonight. You're staying here.'

Moving with a swiftness that took her by surprise, he grabbed the suitcase, tipped it over and all the clothes fell out of it on to the floor. Scooping up the clothes, he flung them into the cupboard, letting them fall anyhow, then he flung both cases on top of them and slid the doors shut, standing in front of them.

'You're not leaving,' he reiterated arrogantly.

'But you can't make me stay,' she retorted, slipping her feet into her sandals. 'There's no way you can make me stay if I don't want to. I can go without my clothes. All I need is my handbag. Oh, where is it?' She looked around the room rather wildly, then suddenly remembering where she had left it she started towards the door. She pulled it open and ran through the sitting room to the passageway.

To the silent, dimly lit hallway she hurried. The handbag wasn't where she had left it. Nor was it anywhere else in the hallway, and she couldn't leave without it; she couldn't go where she would have gone if she could have left, she realised, her shoulders slumping with weariness as she left the hallway and trailed back along the passageway. She couldn't go to St John's to spend the night in a hotel there, and she couldn't fly back to England tomorrow without money and passport.

She would have to wait until tomorrow morning in the hope that Jeremiah had picked up her handbag and put it in a safe place. Yes, she would wait until morning. Right now she was too tired, too emotionally exhausted to go anywhere.

About to enter the sitting room, she met Craig coming out, fully dressed now in hip-hugging dark pants and a thin oatmeal-coloured V-necked sweater which drew attention to the strong column of his neck. He pulled up short when he saw her.

'What? Not gone yet?' he jeered.

'Not going,' she whispered. 'I . . . I can't find my handbag. I left it on a chair in the hall before I went down to the beach and I can't go without it.' Straightening her shoulders, she tilted her chin and looked him straight in the eyes. 'You see, I had no intention of going to the hotel and spending the night with Lyn. I was going to St John's. I've never stayed the night with him. I'm not having an affair with him. I've never lived with him—and what's more, I don't want to,' she added defiantly, as if making a declaration of war.

Eyes narrow, dark face taut, Craig stared at her suspiciously for a moment. Then slowly his expression relaxed. The line of his mouth softened and the ice in his eyes melted.

'Okay I believe you,' he told her. 'And I'm sorry for what I said just now about you running to him.' He paused and his eyes began to glitter again. His lips grew tight. 'But I'm not going to apologise for what happened on the beach,' he added. 'I wanted you and you wanted me. We've wanted each other ever since we met at the airport . . .'

'No, that's not true,' she whispered, backing away from him.

'Yes, it is true. Why the hell do you think I followed when you sailed away with those friends of yours?' he demanded, stepping towards her. 'You're my wife, I'd met you again after being separated from you for two years and I wanted to make love to you . . . a natural, primitive reaction, if you like, but I'm not ashamed of it.' He broke off, frowning, and drew a deep sighing breath. He raised a hand as if to reach out and touch her, then changed his mind and let it drop to his side, his lips twisting wryly. 'Okay, okay,' he sighed. 'You needn't back off—I'm not going to touch you again. So you can't leave without your handbag? I expect Jeremiah has put it somewhere safe. Would you like me to go and ask him where it is? He and Elena have gone to bed, I guess, but I'll go over and knock on their door, if you like.'

'Oh, no, please don't disturb them. I'll get it in the morning.' She smiled rather wanly and pushed a heavy lock of hair back from her face. 'As you said, I won't be going anywhere tonight . . . Except to bed.'

'So why don't you do that?' he suggested quietly, and turned away from her towards the doorway leading to the passageway. 'You can have the bedroom to yourself,' he added. 'I'll find somewhere else to sleep. Goodnight.'

And he walked out of the room, closing the door behind him.

CHAPTER SEVEN

AND so after all Samantha spent the night alone, a tormented, almost sleepless night, eventually falling asleep heavily towards morning. When she awoke the sun was high and she guessed the time to be about ten o'clock by the slant of the shadows.

She knew that Craig had been in the bedroom before she had woken up, because the clothes closet doors were open and the pants and sweater he had worn last night were thrown across a chair. In the bathroom the mirror was still steamed up from the heat of the shower and the towels had been tossed about.

After showering she dressed in white cotton shorts and a thin dark blue shirt which she selected from the heap of clothes in the closet that still lay where Craig had thrown them the night before. After hanging all the clothes up again, wondering vaguely why she wasn't packing them in the suitcase—her mind was still a little numb from lack of sleep—she went out by the patio window and walked across the pool area to the breakfast room window.

The sun shone, the sky was blue, birds were singing and the water in the swimming pool was a cool limpid green. The flowers of the shrubs, golden bells of allamanda, scarlet trumpets of Chinese hibiscus, delicate pink and white frangipani, gaudy, aggressive red and purple bougainvillaea had all been freshly washed by last evening's rain and seemed to glow more brightly than ever.

The table in the breakfast room was still set, but only for one. Jeremiah appeared almost as soon as Samantha entered the room, to wish her good morning and to offer her fresh fruit, either juicy cubes of melon and pineapple combined in a fruit cup; small ripe bananas sliced with fresh cream; or slices of orange and grapefruit.

She chose bananas and cream, to be followed by a poached egg on toast and coffee, then asked Jeremiah if he had found her handbag.

'Yes, ma'am. I gave it to Mr Craig this morning when he asked me about it.'

'Oh. Do you know where he is now?'

'I think he's with Mr Howard, ma'am.'

'Thank you.'

As soon as she had finished eating Samantha went to Howard Clifton's suite of rooms and knocked on the door of the sitting room. Carla's voice called to her to come in.

Carla and Howard were both still sitting at the round breakfast table which was close to the wide open patio window. Bright morning sunlight shafted into the room and small birds were flying about, some of them tame enough to perch on the edge of the table cheekily looking for crumbs. Craig wasn't in the room.

'Good morning Samantha. You are looking well this morning,' said Carla in her usual warm and welcoming way. 'Have you had breakfast yet?'

'Yes, thank you. I'm looking for Craig, Jeremiah said he was here with you.'

'He left a few minutes ago,' said Howard. 'He's gone down to the Dockyard. Didn't he tell you?'

To see Morgana, whispered a small voice in Samantha's mind. She shut it out instantly. She had no reason to be jealous of Morgana—no reason at all. Craig had said so.

'No, he didn't,' she admitted. 'I . . . I slept in this morning. He must have gone before I woke up. Did he say when he'd be back?'

'Around lunchtime,' said Carla, rising to her feet. 'If you'll excuse me, Howard, I wish to speak with Elena about the luncheon. I'll send Jeremiah to clear the table.' She bent over him and kissed him on the cheek, then went towards the door.

'No, don't go, Samantha,' ordered Howard when she would have followed Carla from the room. 'Come out to the patio and walk with me for a while. There are a few matters I want to talk to you about. Did you find out where that rumour started?'

'Yes, I did,' she replied, going over to him and handing him the silver-knobbed cane which he always leaned on when walking. He looked better this morning than he had yesterday afternoon, she thought, and his eyes were bright and shrewd as they appraised her. Slowly, together they stepped out on to the sunlit stone flags. The air was scented by the many roses that were growing in the flower beds. From far below came the sound of the sea whispering among the rocks. 'I went to see Lyndon . . . the journalist who interviewed you . . . and asked him where he'd heard the rumour, and he said a woman who was staying at the Admiral's Inn told him. From the description he gave of her I guessed it was Morgana Taylor.'

'Aha!' drawled Howard. 'And where do you think she picked up the information?'

'I have no idea. Unless . ._' Samantha broke off, not liking the thought which had just sprung into her mind. 'Unless Craig told her,' she went on. 'He told me last night that he knows I'd consulted a lawyer in London about a divorce, but I don't know how he can have found out.'

'He knows because I told him,' said Howard crisply.

'When?' exclaimed Samantha. 'When did you tell him?'

'I told him as soon as I received the information from London,' he replied coolly.

'Oh, I don't understand,' exclaimed Samantha, thoroughly bewildered by now. 'I didn't tell anyone I'd been to see a lawyer except Lyndon Barry, and since he didn't know I'm married to Craig until yesterday he couldn't possibly have told you. Who told you? How did you find out?'

They had reached the railing at the far end of the patio and Howard stopped to look out at the view of the bay and the sea beyond shimmering under the morning sunlight. Beside him Samantha studied his hawklike profile. A cunning old man, Lyndon had called him.

'I was informed by certain people in London who work for the company and who have kept an eye on you ever since you decided to live separately from Craig,' he replied coldly.

'Spied on me, don't you mean?' she retorted, horrified by what he had said. 'Oh, how could you?'

'You can call it spying if you like,' he replied smoothly, not at all put out by the accusation, and flicked an icy glance in her direction. 'I may as well tell you now that Craig married you to defy me. At the time Conrad Taylor and I were discussing the merger of our two companies, and we hoped to cement that merger by a marriage between Craig and Morgana. In fact Conrad made the marriage the only condition on which he would agree to a merger. Craig refused to co-operate and went off to England and married you. Since you did not come from a wealthy family I was not unnaturally suspicious of you, believing you to have married him for his wealth and position. When, after not much more than a year of marriage, you returned to England and insisted on taking a job there it seemed to me that my suspicions had been confirmed, so I had you watched. As I told you yesterday, I didn't want you to do to Craig what Ashley did to me, and as soon as I heard you'd been to see a lawyer I decided to take action.'

'What action?'

'I invited you to come out here, of course,' he replied, 'after first making sure that you were relieved of your position on *Woman's Insight* so that you wouldn't have the excuse of saying you couldn't come out here because you were working.'

'So it was you who put pressure on Marilyn Dowell!' she gasped.

'I do not put pressure,' he retorted coldly. 'I give orders and make sure they are obeyed.'

'But I might not have accepted your invitation,' Samantha replied spiritedly. 'Then what would you have done?'

'But you did accept my invitation,' he said silkily. 'You came, and as I had hoped, so did Craig come as soon as he knew you were here, and yesterday you told me yourself that your separation from him is over and that there isn't going to be a divorce.' His lips tilted up at the corners. 'And I'm very pleased that my little plan to get you and Craig together has worked and also that I've had the opportunity of getting to know you better. You see, my dear, during the past week while you've been staying here I've come to realise you didn't marry Craig for his money. You married him because you fell in love with him, didn't you?'

'I . . . how did you find out?' she muttered.

'By listening to you and watching you, and also because you didn't hesitate to accept my invitation to come and see me,' he said. 'You were hoping to hear something about him while you were here and possibly you hoped to meet him here, weren't you?'

'Yes, I was,' she admitted in a whisper.

'You were getting just a little tired of being separated from him, but you didn't want to be the one to make the first move and he didn't seem to be making any move at all. So you went to see a lawyer about a divorce, hoping to jolt Craig into making a move—and you did. When I told him over the phone that I'd heard you'd been to see a divorce lawyer he wanted to fly to England immediately. But I suggested that you met him here, away from certain influences in your life he had told me about. He tells me that your mother has never approved of him any more than I've approved of you.'

'She thinks he has a playboy mentality towards women and that he married me only to . . . well, to . . .'

'Get you into his bed,' Howard finished for her

dryly, a twinkle beginning to dance in the depths of his eyes. 'Well, I don't blame him for that. You're an extremely attractive woman, a little mixed up in your thinking, perhaps, but interesting and challenging, not one of those submissive women, thank God, and ideally suited to Craig, I would think. He's a bit too inclined to ride roughshod over people to get his own way and you're right to stand up to him. So there it is, Samantha, now you know what a crafty old man I am, pulling strings behind the scenes and manipulating people. Am I forgiven for spying on you, giving you the sack and inviting you to come out here? I did it all for the best, you know.'

'Yes, you're forgiven,' she said with a sigh. 'But since you've been honest with me I think I should be honest with you. Craig and I are only pretending that our separation is over.'

'Pretending?'

'Yes. He asked me to pretend it's over for a few days.'

'Did he tell you why?'

'No, but I had the impression it was to please you.'

'And you had no objection to going along with this . . . this pretence?'

'No . . . at least . . . I . . .' Samantha broke off, realising that she didn't really know why she had agreed to Craig's suggestion.

'Perhaps you decided that half a cake is better than none,' said Howard, the twinkle dancing in his eyes again. 'And you're right, it is. So how long is this pretence to go on?'

'No longer than a week, he said.'

'And when the week is over?'

'I can go back to London if I want to.'

'If you want to. Mmm. It seems that Craig is capable of being more subtle than I've given him credit for,' Howard mused. 'Maybe he's learned a thing or two from his father, after all. It's just possible that you won't want to go back to London, isn't it?'

'Yes, I suppose it is,' Samantha muttered.

'And if you don't go back there, what then?' he pressed her, leaning towards her his lips twisted into a mocking smile.

'Oh, I . . . I don't know,' she replied rather wildly. 'I just don't know. It . . . it will depend on what Craig does. Please will you excuse me now? I have to look for something I couldn't find yesterday evening.'

'Yes, you're excused, but I'll expect to see you later this evening,' said Howard autocratically as they walked back towards his sitting room. 'I'm making a date with you now for later. You haven't read to me for some time, and we're half way through Hemingway's *The Old Man and the Sea*. I want to know what happens in the end, so don't you go running off to sea or anywhere else before you've finished reading it to me. Promise?'

'Yes, I promise,' she replied. 'I'll be here this evening.'

Leaving him, she went straight to her own rooms to search for her handbag, sure that Craig must have put it somewhere where she could see it. But she couldn't find it anywhere, neither in the bedroom nor the sitting room, and that meant she couldn't leave Antigua today, at least she couldn't leave until Craig returned to the house and she was able to ask him for the handbag.

She was trapped again. Not that it mattered, she thought, with a new yet strange sense of relief because the matter had been taken out of her hands. She hadn't really wanted to leave and she had more or less decided to stay for the rest of the week Craig had asked her to stay for. Then she would leave, if she wanted to.

It's just possible you won't want to, isn't it? Howard Clifton had suggested. Oh, what a sharp and cunning mind he had! How well he had studied her and had analysed her behaviour. He seemed to know more about her than she did herself and had guessed accurately at the motive that had sent her scurrying to her lawyer for advice about a divorce. When the two years Craig had stipulated as the length of their separation had been over and there had been no sign or word from him about ending it, she had been desperate and had intended to ask the lawyer to get in touch with Craig, suggesting a divorce in the hope—as Howard had so rightly guessed—of jolting Craig into taking some action. But before she had been able to do that Howard had been informed of what she had done and had acted. She had been sacked from her job on his instructions and had received the invitation to fly out to Antigua. As Lyn had put it, she had been duped—and very easily duped at that—into coming here and meeting Craig again.

And Craig had come here because he had known she would be here, he had made no secret of that. He had followed her through the islands when she had run away with the Wallises because he had wanted to make love to her. He had asked her to come back with him and to pretend their separation was over, but he had only asked her to pretend after she had suggested that was what he wanted. She frowned and bit her lip. Was it possible she had misunderstood him and that he had really been asking her to resume their marriage properly? No, she didn't think so, because he had stipulated a time limit—a few days, possibly no longer than a week, then she could go back to London if she wanted. He wouldn't have done that, surely, if he wanted her to go back to him.

But why had he wanted her to pretend their separation was over? Was it just to please his father, as Lyn had suggested? Or was there some other reason? She was no nearer to knowing. But did she have to know? Couldn't she pretend their separation was over because he loved her and wanted her back? And if she pretended hard enough couldn't she make the pretence a reality?

Stripping off her shorts and shirt, she pulled on a swimsuit, draped a terry-towelling beach robe over it and left the room. She would go windsurfing. The weather was just right for skimming across the waters of the little bay, the wind light but steady, the sunshine warm. It would be better than sitting about trying to analyse the situation between herself and Craig; better than wondering what he was doing at the Dockyard; wondering if he was with Morgana.

For the next half hour she flitted back and forth across the bay, trying to improve her ability at sailing to windward, pleased with herself for not capsizing once. Feeling pleasantly refreshed by the exercise, she guided the little sail craft over to her favourite beach, intending to rest there for a while and sunbathe before going back to the house for lunch and to see Craig.

Taking the chance of being alone in an isolated place to sunbathe in the nude, she stripped off her *maillot* and placed it on a rock to dry, then lay down on the warm sand on her back, closing her eyes. The peace and quiet were heavenly. The sun was just right, not too hot, caressing her skin and colouring those parts of her that weren't usually exposed with a golden tan, she hoped. The water whispered and glugged among the nearby rocks. The leaves of sea-grapes rattled together as the wind touched them. Peace, perfect peace in a place where no one else came.

'Do you come here often?'

Samantha opened her eyes quickly and sat up in alarm, covering her breasts with her arms. She looked around but saw no one. The beach was deserted, no other windsurfer was drawn up by hers. No tall man, his skin glittering with drops of water, was standing beside her either. She looked behind at the cliffs. No one up there.

Standing up, she picked up her *maillot* and pulled it on, just in case there was someone hiding among the rocks and peeping at her, then she lay down again, this time on her stomach, pillowing her head on her folded arms. She closed her eyes, hoping again to feel the peacefulness of the place seeping into her mind, soothing it.

But peace of mind had gone and would no longer be possible in that place. It was haunted by Craig; by his voice, deep and soft, mocking her. She was haunted by him and she always would be, and now she found she was aching for him to be there with her, wishing that she had really heard

his voice and not just imagined hearing it. If only
he would come, following her across the bay. If
only he were there, tanned skin glowing, grey
glance flashing over her in appreciation of the way
she looked; white teeth glinting in that mocking,
provocative grin; lean hands reaching out and
touching her, stroking her, holding her. Oh, how
much she wanted him! Her hands clenched and she
groaned in an agony of desire.

She couldn't stay there any longer. She had to
get back to Cliff House to see him, to find him if
he wasn't there, to tell him she wanted to stop
pretending their separation was over. She wanted
to tell him she loved him and was willing to live
with him again, always and for ever. Jumping to
her feet, she ran down to the windsurfer. Quickly
she fitted the mast, pushed the board out into the
water, stepped on to it and was away, with the
wide sail filling with wind and the water chuckling
crisply.

Reaching the beach below Cliff House, she
begrudged the time she had to spend carrying the
windsurfer board and the mast and sail to the
racks where they were always stored. She just
couldn't move quickly enough to keep up with her
desire to see Craig again, to talk to him, to touch
him and to make her confession of love. Her beach
robe was where she had left it on the rack, and she
pulled it on, tying it at her waist, then thrust her
feet into her sandals.

She ran to the steps and began to run up them,
pulling herself up by the rail that ran along one
side of them, but halfway up she ran out of
breath and had to pause on the wooden platform
where there was a rough bench on which to rest

and where the steps changed direction, turning to the left for the final ascent to the top of the cliff.

Samantha had caught her breath and she was just about to continue the climb when the click of high heels on the steps made her look up and draw back sharply. A vision in a blue voile dress scattered all over with sequins was coming down towards her. White-blonde ringlets danced about a thin triangular face. Morgana reached the platform and stood before Samantha, effectively blocking the way up the steps, and showing her small white teeth in a falsely sweet smile.

'Hi. Carla said you might be on the beach, so I came down to find you,' she drawled. Her dark eyes opened wide as their glance roved over Samantha's wet hair. 'What on earth have you been doing?' she exclaimed. 'You look half drowned!'

'I've been windsurfing.'

'Oh. Are you any good at it?'

'Not bad. Have you ever tried it?'

'Good God, no!' Morgana gave a little shudder. 'I dislike any form of water sports. I don't like to get wet.'

'Like a cat,' Samantha couldn't help remarking, and Morgana gave her a coolly vicious sidelong glance. 'Excuse me, please, I'd like to go up to the house now to have a shower and to change,' Samantha added.

'Not yet,' said Morgana, not moving out of the way. 'We can talk here just as well as anywhere else, and I have a lot to say to you. Where did you learn to windsurf?'

'Craig taught me when we were on our honeymoon,' said Samantha. 'But please say what it is you want to say and then I can go and change. Is it important?'

'It is to me,' replied Morgana tautly, her lips thinning, stretching out both arms and resting her hands on the railings that bordered the flight of steps behind her. To go past her Samantha would have to knock one of her arms down if Morgana wouldn't move out of the way. 'I really don't know why you're hanging in the way you are,' the other woman went on,' her eyes beginning to glitter unpleasantly.

'Hanging in? Whatever do you mean?' asked Samantha with a little laugh.

'Staying on here, then,' Morgana snapped. 'Hanging around, thinking you're going to get Craig back by being here, putting yourself in his way, reminding him all the time that he's legally bound to you. You know, I'm really surprised at you.' Her red lips twisted into a sneer. 'I thought you had more spunk than to put up with the way he behaves. You know, I actually cheered when I heard you'd decided to separate from him. I felt you'd struck a blow on behalf of feminism, refusing to be domineered over by him. But I'd have thought by now you'd have gone ahead and divorced him and taken what you could from him in the way of a good settlement.'

'I've no doubt that's what you'd have done if you'd found yourself in my position,' Samantha sniped, but her voice shook slightly. She wasn't very good at sniping.

'You're darned right, I would. And I was sure that was what you would do,' retorted Morgana. 'So sure that you've been spreading a rumour to that effect!'

'I have mentioned it to some of the Mill Reef crowd, yes,' replied Morgana with a slight shrug of her shoulders. 'Some of them are friends of mine and Craig's. And they've asked me how things are with his marriage because they know he and I are so close.' The dark eyes were narrow now, and watching Samantha.

'Then it must have been quite a setback to your credibility among your friends when you heard from Craig that we've ended our separation and that there's to be no divorce,' replied Samantha, her head up, her eyes steady, although she was beginning to shake all over, she discovered, she was so angry with this woman, and she had to push her hands into the pockets of her robe and clench them into fists, she was so afraid she might hit Morgana.

Immediately Morgana's attitude changed. Heavy white lids hid her dark eyes and letting go of the railings she sighed a little as she stepped towards Samantha.

'Oh, my dear,' she breathed gently, 'I feel so sorry for you! You're so gullible, so easily-misled. You're no match for a man like Craig. He's too sophisticated, too wordly-wise for someone like you. I can imagine how he would talk you out of divorcing him and into ending the separation. And he would be encouraged to do that by his father because Howard wouldn't want you divorcing his son and demanding a big settlement. He hates to lose money that way. I wouldn't put it past Howard to even offer to pay you to pretend your separation from Craig is over. In other words, to buy you off.'

'Well, you're wrong, he hasn't,' said Samantha,

clenching her hands even harder, her voice cracking slightly she was so furious. 'Would you please let me pass now,' she went on, stepping to one side of Morgana in an attempt to get by and go up the steps, but Morgana sidestepped too and was still there in front of her, smiling her falsely sweet smile.

'Then it's worse than I'd thought,' she whispered insinuatingly. 'They've talked you into it.' She sighed again. 'You're making a terrible mistake, you know, and I did so hope you'd learned from your first mistake.'

'What was that?' Samantha couldn't help asking.

'Marrying Craig, of course. I suppose you fell for that clean-cut look of his, for his apparent openness and honesty, heady stuff when combined with wealth, an ability to excel at dangerous sports and a reputuation as a financial whiz-kid. I suppose he seemed like Prince Charming to you, come to rescue you from the poverty of being Cinderella.'

'He did not!' retorted Samantha spiritedly. 'I'm not like Cinderella, and I've never lived in poverty.'

'But you did believe you would live happily ever after with Craig when you married him, didn't you?' sighed Morgana. 'So naïve of you—I find it incredible that there are still women like you around. And how you can continue to believe like that in the face of reality, I don't know. I suppose you think too that Craig has been faithful to you during the past two years you've been separated from him. Well, I can assure you he hasn't, and you could very easily divorce him on those grounds.'

'I ... I don't want to hear any more!' cried
Samantha, and stepped sideways the other way to
the outside of the platform. 'Let me get past,' she
muttered, and would have pushed by Morgana
forcibly. Her hand in fact did actually go out and
she felt it contact Morgana's bare sun-warmed
arm. That arm lifted, suddenly and resentfully
shaking off her hand. Samantha had a glimpse of
Morgana's face, twisted with fury, the dark eyes
seeming to flicker with little red flames, and then
somehow she was falling backwards.

Desperately she tried to keep her balance and
failed. There was nothing behind her but the steps
leading down to the other platform several yards
below. She felt herself twisting through the air. She
heard herself screaming. Everything was rushing
past her, whirling around, rocks, shrubs, clinging
trees. She crashed against something at last, she
didn't know what, and lost consciousness.

It was a long time before she became fully
conscious again, and when she did she was lying
on the bed in her bedroom in the house and she
felt bruised all over. The room was almost dark
and she wondered how she came to be there. It
was an effort to think because her head hurt so
much, but she remembered she had been windsurfing, and then it had become suddenly urgent to see
Craig, to find him and to tell him something. Had
she found him and told him? The effort to remember
was too great. Her mind was growing hazy again.
How had she got here? She couldn't remember
walking into the house. All she could remember was
coming ashore in the windsurfer, putting it away,
going up the steps and meeting Morgana.

Morgana getting in the way, stopping her from

going on to the house to find Craig. Morgana always between her and Craig. Morgana tormenting her, baiting her. Morgana pushing her when she had tried to pass; pushing her back until she had lost her balance and had fallen backwards!

'Oh, no!' The groan was a faint sound in the room, but it was heard, and someone came to the side of the bed.

'Samantha!'

Craig's voice. She had found him at last. Now what was it she had to tell him? She opened her eyes, tried to raise her head. Pain, sharp and excruciating, shot through her neck and she cried out.

'No, don't move.' He sat down on the bed beside her. His face floated into her vision, hovered above her, dark except for the glint of his eyes. 'You mustn't move until the doctor has come and has examined you,' he said quietly. 'I took a risk carrying you up here when I found you. Do you know what happened? How did you fall? Did you trip?'

'No.' Her throat was dry and it was difficult to speak, to make her lips form the shape of the words. 'I met Morgana. She ... she wouldn't let me get past her. I tried to step around her and ... and I must have lost my balance ...' Her voice trailed away to nothing.

'Morgana?' He sounded puzzled. 'Are you sure you met her?'

'Yes.' The sound was like a sigh, no more.

'But she left Antigua this morning,' he said. 'Her father told me this morning that she'd left when I went to see him.' He bent closer to her, raised his hand and pressed his fingers against her forehead, all the time looking at her eyes closely. Samantha wanted to argue with him to tell him he was wrong and that Morgana had been at Cliff House that day, but the words wouldn't come. 'I think you must have a fever,' he told her. 'Perhaps you're delirious and imagining you saw Morgana.' He glanced sideways at the door and taking his hand from her brow stood up. 'This must be the doctor now,' he said, and walked away out of her view.

Dr Williams, who attended Howard Clifton regularly, was a pleasant Antiguan who had done his medical training in England. He examined her gently and pronounced that she was lucky enough not to have broken a leg or her pelvis or her back As it was she had a badly sprained wrist, many bad bruises, concussion, and was suffering mostly from severe shock.

'If you like I can arrange to have her moved to the hospital and treated there,' he said to Craig.

'No!' Samantha tried to speak and couldn't. She stared at Craig intently, not daring to shake her head negatively in case it hurt again but trying to convey to him that she didn't want to go to the hospital among strange people. She wanted to stay where he was. He got the message and turned to the doctor.

'We can look after her here, I'm sure, if you tell us what to do,' he said. 'Can't we, Carla?' he added, looking across the bed at Carla, who had accompanied the doctor into the room.

'But of course. She will have every attention.' Carla stepped forward so that Samantha could see her. 'We will look after, you, *querida*, never fear, and in a few days' time you'll be as good as new.'

But more than a few days passed before Samantha felt anywhere near as good as new. A whole week passed before she was able to move without too much pain and before she was able to speak properly, think coherently and remember everything that had happened the day she had fallen; before she remembered why she had been returning to the house to find Craig; before she remembered what she had been going to say to him.

The morning that she remembered she awakened feeling rested and clear-headed for the first time and she looked forward to seeing him. All the time, all the days and nights of alternately dozing and waking, of being in pain and being without pain under the influence of pain-killing drugs, she had been aware of him in the bedroom, mostly sitting in the chair beside the bed; sometimes not speaking at all to her, as if he sensed she didn't want to talk; sometimes reading to her from a magazine or a newspaper; sometimes passing on messages to her from Howard. Once he had told her how he had found her lying unconscious on the steps. She had been missed at lunchtime by Carla, who had told him she had last been seen windsurfing, so he had gone down to the beach to look for her.

And then she had tried to tell him again about Morgana and how she was sure the woman had pushed her. He had listened, but Samantha had been able to tell he hadn't believed her because he had stopped her and had urged her to rest again and not to talk, speaking to her gently and authoritatively as if she were a child and then leaving the room, his place being taken by the nurse he had hired to look after her or by Carla.

But today she was strong enough to argue with him and to insist that Morgana had been with her when she had fallen, and when he came she wouldn't be lying in bed, at a disadvantage. She would be up and properly dressed and sitting in the chair, proving to him that she was no longer delirious from the slight concussion she had suffered, nor was she hallucinating from the pain-killers. She wasn't an invalid any more. She was a convalescent and well on the way to recovery, so Craig would have to believe what she had to tell him about Morgana. She hoped, too, that he would believe her when she told him why she had been looking for him; when she told him she loved him and wanted to end their separation for ever.

The nurse was reluctant to allow her up, but after a while gave in to persuasion, and by the time Carla came into the room to check on her progress Samantha was sitting by the open patio window watching the sunlight dappling the water in the pool and enjoying the feel of the sun's warmth on her face.

'I feel so much better,' she explained to Carla. 'I just had to get up. Is Craig about? I would like to see him. I have such a lot to tell him now that I feel well again.'

The expression on Carla's large heavy-featured face changed with almost comical swiftness from sincere smiling delight in Samantha's obvious improvement to mouth-drooping sadness.

'Ah, I am so sorry, *querida*, that he is not here, for I know how much he had wanted you to get better, how many hours he has sat in this room with you while you slept at night, keeping watch over you in case you wakened and wanted something or in case you felt ill.'

'Not here? Oh, has he gone out to English Harbour or to St John's?' asked Samantha, trying hard to hide her disappointment.

'No. He has gone back to Toronto,' replied Carla.

'Gone already?' exclaimed Samantha. 'But the flight to Toronto doesn't leave until later in the afternoon. It has to come from Toronto first.'

'He went on yesterday afternoon's flight,' replied Carla, looking puzzled. 'But I'm sure he must have told you, *querida*, when he was with you. He had his lunch with you, don't you remember?'

They were always doubting her ability to remember now, she had noticed, she thought rather irritably, as if she suffered from amnesia as a result of the fall.

'Yes, I remember. But he didn't say he was going away . . .' Samantha broke off as she tried to remember exactly what Craig had said to her when he had left her the previous afternoon. 'He said . . . he wouldn't be having dinner with me so I was not to expect to see him in the evening because he wouldn't be here,' she murmured, talking to herself more than to Carla, finding that if she talked her thoughts were not so muddled. 'He said too that he'd already stayed longer than he should.'

'That is right,' said Carla, nodding her head. 'He came for only a short time to see you while you were here and then when you were hurt he didn't want to leave you. But now he has had to go back to attend to some business. It is always the way with him—business, business, business,' she added. 'Howard used to be the same. I never knew when he was going or when he was coming. But now that part is over. He has to stay in one place more. It is much nicer for me. And it will happen for you too one day.' She patted Samantha's shoulder comfortingly. 'So you see, Craig did tell you he was going away.'

'I suppose he did, in a way,' admitted Samantha, her eyes filling with tears suddenly. 'But I can't help wishing . . .' Again she broke off as waves of weakness and disappointment washed over her.

'You get up too soon,' Carla chided her. 'You think your strength come back all at once. Now come and lie down again on the bed, rest some more, and then later this afternoon you can get up again.'

Suddenly dispirited, Samantha allowed Carla to lead her to the bed. She lay down obediently and closed her eyes. The pretence was over. Craig had gone back to Toronto and it was no longer necessary to pretend their separation was over. For a few days, possibly no longer than a week, the pretence had lasted, and then a little longer, because she had fallen and hurt herself and he had felt honour bound to stay and make sure she recovered. It had all been part of the pretence. But now he had gone, leaving as usual, abruptly, without saying goodbye, without saying where he was going, leaving her free to return to London if she wanted.

CHAPTER EIGHT

A week later, not having heard from Craig and resisting Carla's and Howard's insistence that she should stay longer at Cliff House until she was fully recovered, Samantha flew from Antigua to London.

There was no one to meet her at Heathrow, which was not surprising because she hadn't told anyone that she would be returning that day. From the airport she phoned Thea Johnson, her friend from schooldays with whom she had been sharing a flat before she had gone out to Antigua. A little rushed, since it was early morning and she was just preparing to leave for work, Thea welcomed Samantha back and said yes, it would be fine for her to move back into the flat; her belongings were still there and no one had taken her place.

'Because you did say you'd be back, you know,' Thea said brightly. 'You've got a key, haven't you?'

'Yes.'

'Then just come straight here. I'll see you later tonight—much later, because I'm going out with a friend after work, and you can tell me about your holiday then. I bet you have a gorgeous tan. Must go now 'Bye!'

Struggling with her suitcases, Samantha made her way to the Underground and was soon being whisked away from the airport into London. An hour and a half later, feeling exhausted after the long flight and subsequent journey complicated by two changes of route on the Underground to reach the area of the metropolis where she lived, she walked into the small flat. It looked exactly the same as when she had left it . . . how long ago? Standing just inside the door, her brow furrowed, she tried to remember how long she had been away. It seemed like a year, but it was in fact barely a month.

Not bothering to unpack, she went to bed and slept most of the day. When she wakened it was late afternoon and after making herself a meal she phoned her parents to tell them she had returned. She said nothing about having seen Craig while she had been away. She didn't want to get into an argument with her mother about him. The less her mother knew about the complications of her relationship with Craig, the better, she thought.

She said nothing about him to Thea either, but talked only about the beauty of the islands she had sailed among; about the Wallises and some of the other people she had met.

'Mm sounds like paradise to me,' sighed Thea. 'Maybe I should start saving up to take a trip out there next year. What are you going to do now?'

'Look for a job,' replied Samantha.

'You're not going to find it easy, especially in your line of work.'

And she didn't find it easy, and by the end of her first week back in England, although she had had several interviews she hadn't been offered a job. Then on the Friday morning, just as she was thinking of packing a bag and going down to Epping to stay for the weekend with her parents, she received a surprise telephone call.

'Marilyn Dowell here, Samantha. How are you?'

'Fine, thank you. And you?'

'Mustn't grumble. Did you enjoy your holiday in Antigua?'

'Yes, I did, but how did you know I've been out there?'

'Oh, I must have heard it from someone in the office,' replied Marilyn vaguely. 'Samantha, I was wondering, are you working?'

'No. I wouldn't be here in the flat on a Friday morning if I was, would I?'

'I suppose not. How would you like to come back to *Woman's Insight*?'

'In what capacity?' asked Samantha cautiously.

'Same as before.'

'What happened to the cutback for economic reasons?' asked Samantha dryly.

'Oh, that? We've found out that it didn't work,' Marilyn was still vague. 'So how about it, Samantha? Like to start on Monday?'

'I . . . I'll have to think about it. I . . . I . . . have had other offers. Could I get back to you?'

'Of course. Any time. Nice talking to you,' replied Marilyn, apparently not at all offended by Samantha's refusal, and she rang off.

There was no doubt in Samantha's mind that Marilyn had been instructed to offer her a job by someone among the top brass of Clifton Enterprises. By Howard or by Craig? Why? She didn't want to know and she wasn't going to think about it, as she had said she would. She was going away for the weekend and she was going to forget all about her immediate problems.

Much to her relief, her parents were too taken up with arranging and attending the christening of their first grandchild to enquire too probingly about her holiday or about her personal life, and she was soon involved in helping her mother to prepare the food that would be served at the party after the baby, a bouncing blue-eyed boy, had been been christened in the local church. Then there were walks in the woods with her father and the dogs, drives to the local shopping mall to buy extras that Brenda Lewis had forgotten. In fact Saturday and Sunday both went by so quickly that she was on the Underground train returning to London before she realised she hadn't told her sister Jennifer that she had met Pam Wallis while she had been in Antigua and had gone cruising with her and her husband Ken.

It all seemed like a dream, now, she thought as she walked along the street where she lived with Thea; as if those days of sunshine, blue skies and blue water, yellow sands and palm trees hadn't been; as if she had imagined them. If only she had; if only she hadn't really been to Antigua, hadn't really sailed to the other islands, hadn't really been followed by Craig and sailed back with him on a beautiful moonlit night to Antigua, she wouldn't have these painful memories of having been with him. She wouldn't be hurting because she wanted to be with him again.

Reaching the house where the flat was, she entered the narrow hallway and climbed the stairs to the second floor and then to the third floor. Sounds of music, of TV voices, came through closed doors as she went up. She was just inserting the key into the lock on the door of her flat—an awkward business because the key didn't quite fit and had to be jiggled in—when the door was opened by Thea. She was wearing outdoor clothes, a thick woollen cape, designed to keep out the chill of March winds, and she stood in the doorway solidly blocking the way, her eyes bright as they fixed on Samantha's, as if she were trying to flash messages.

'You have a visitor,' she whispered. 'From Canada.'

'Wh-who?' whispered Samantha, her eyes widening, her heart beginning to thump.

'Can't you guess?' hissed Thea.

'Wh-when did he come?'

'This afternoon. I couldn't get him to leave. He said he'd wait until you got back.'

'But how . . . how did he know where to come?' asked Samantha.

'I don't know. I'll leave you to find that out.'

'I . . . I don't want to see him,' said Samantha, in sudden panic, turning away towards the stairs, but Thea caught hold of her arm. 'Please tell him, Thea!'

'You must. He hasn't come several thousand miles to be put off by me. He's here to see you, and . . .' Thea's lips quirked in a knowledgeable grin, 'well, he's really something else, isn't he? Seems to me you're a bit of a fool if you don't talk it out with him, come to some compromise.'

'But you don't understand,' muttered Samantha, glancing nervously over Thea's shoulder, trying to see into the lamplit living room and failing.

'Oh, yes, I do. I understand very well,' whispered Thea. 'You're in love with each other, but you're both too damned proud to admit it.'

Somehow, Samantha wasn't quite sure how it happened, she was inside the room and Thea was

behind her, still standing in the open doorway.
Standing straight, her face pale, one hand fidgeting
nervously with the strap of her holdall which was
slung over her shoulder, she saw Craig get up from
the sofa where he had been sitting and come
towards her. He was dressed very differently from
the last time she had seen him, in tweed pants and
a thick brown and cream sweater with Eskimo
deisgns all over it, but his manner wasn't changed.
Coolly self-confident, his grey eyes cold and
wintery in his sunbrowned lean face, advanced
like a predator stalking its prey. Samantha's
nerves twanged and she turned as if to run from
the room, but Thea was already closing the door.

'Thea!' she exclaimed. 'Don't go—please!'

'Have to, love.' Thea looked back into the
room. 'Got a date. And don't expect me back. I'm
staying the night with a friend. 'Bye!' The door
clicked shut.

'Thea!' Samantha made for the door, but Craig
was there barring the way.

'Oh, no, you don't' he drawled. 'You're staying
here with me. There's a lot you have to explain.'

'There's a lot you have to explain too,' she
retorted, tilting her chin.

'Okay,' he agreed smoothly, reaching out and
lifting her holdall from her shoulder and dropping
it to the floor by the telephone table which was
against the wall just inside the door. 'So we'll talk.'
His eyes narrowed as they took in the paleness of
her face and the strained expression in her eyes,
and the stern straight line of his lips softened. 'But
you're tired,' he said gently. 'Come and sit down,
over here.' Reaching out again, he took hold of
her hand this time and though she thought she

ought to pull it from his grasp, the warm strength of his fingers and palm enfolding hers was so comforting that she didn't resist but let him lead her over to the sofa, where she sat down quickly because her legs had begun to shake in reaction to his presence. 'Can I get you something?' he asked. 'A drink? Something to eat?'

'I've eaten this evening,' Samantha replied woodenly, not looking at him. 'A drink would be nice ... but I'm not sure what we have.'

'Beer and some dregs of sherry, your friend told me,' he said dryly. 'But I have a flask of brandy in my holdall,' he added, with a slight grin. 'You know I never leave home without it,' he went on with a touch of self-mockery. 'Strictly for medicinal purposes, of course.'

'Or in case you find yourself stranded by bad weather somewhere,' she murmured, leaning back against the cushions and closing her eyes. The shared remembrance of the time when she had once asked him why he always carried the flask of brandy about with him was warming too.

'Or in case I have to entertain an attractive woman,' he added. 'Like now.' And she heard him walking away from her in the direction of the kitchen.

She opened her eyes. She could go now, leave while he was busy. She stared at the door of the flat. The distance between her and it seemed to be widening by the second. Too far for her to cover quickly in her present condition. She was too tired; tired of running; tired of running away from love and its demands.

'There don't seem to be any brandy glasses, so we'll have to make do with these wine-glasses,' said Craig, coming back into the room. He offered her a glass that was almost full of tawny liquor.

'That's far too much for me!' she gasped, taking it from him. 'I'll get tight!'

'So? Why worry? You'll be in good company,' he retorted with a wicked glint as he sat down beside her. 'I'll put you to bed.' He raised his glass to her. 'Here's to us,' he toasted, drank some of the brandy and set his glass down on the coffee table. 'You have the first word if you like and tell me why you left Antigua in such a rush,' he added, turning towards her.

'You suggested, if you care to remember, that I might come back to London if I wanted when the time for pretending that our separation was over was ended. And since you'd gone back to Toronto I assumed you didn't want to continue with the pretence any more, so as soon as I felt well enough to travel I came back here,' she replied, and took a sip of her drink. 'But you could have said something before you left Cliff House,' she added in a low voice. 'You could have told me you were leaving and that the pretence was over. Why didn't you?' She looked at him accusingly.

Craig frowned, changed position, picked up his glass, sipped more brandy and leaned forward with his elbows on his knees. That way she couldn't see all his face, only the jut of his jaw, the proud downward curve of his nose, one high cheekbone and the way his Indian-black hair sprang back to curve about one ear and the back of his neck.

'I had to go back to Toronto to attend to some business,' he told her. He drank some more brandy. 'I'd guessed, from the way you behaved after . . .' he paused and drew in a breath, then continued, bitterness rasping in his voice, 'from the way you behaved after I'd made love to you on the beach, that you weren't too keen to go on with the pretence, so I didn't think you'd mind if I left without saying anything. In fact, I got the impression you'd be relieved if I removed myself from your vicinity again.' He tossed off the rest of his drink and put down the glass. 'But I intended to go back to Antigua as soon as I could, to make sure you'd fully recovered from that fall.' He half turned his head and slanted a glance at her over his shoulder. 'And to try again to put an end to our separation,' he added. 'I didn't think you'd be well enough to run away again.' He laughed shortly. 'I was wrong,' he said dryly.

There was a short silence and Samantha realised he wasn't going to say anything else and that he was waiting for her.

'I wasn't relieved when you went away,' she whispered. 'I . . . I was very upset.'

'You were?' He gave her another over-the-shoulder glance. 'Why?'

'Because . . . that day, the day after you'd left, I began to feel much better and I remembered what it was I'd been going to say to you . . . just before I met Morgana and she pushed me down the steps.' She felt shaky again, so she sipped some more brandy. It flowed through her, golden fire easing the tension within her and giving her the courage to speak her mind. 'Oh, but I forgot,' she added acidly. 'You don't believe I saw Morgana that day, do you? You think I imagined she was there and that she pushed me. She's your friend, from childhood days, and you can't believe she would do anything so spiteful.'

Craig didn't make an immediate reply but leaned his head on his hands, thrusting long fingers through his black hair.

'Morgana and I were never all that friendly when we were kids,' he admitted. 'Actually I didn't see much of her until I left university and went to work for Clifton Enterprises. Then she used to follow me about, turn up wherever I was. God, could she talk! And all about herself and what a great writer she was going to be or was already. It got so that I used to panic whenever I saw her.' He paused and dropping his hands turned to look at her again. 'I know for sure now that you didn't imagine she was on the steps that day and she pushed you, but at the time you told me I couldn't understand how she could have been there. I really believed she'd gone off with that man she'd met. She must have called in at Cliff House on the way to the airport. I saw her in Toronto when I returned there.'

'Oh. I see.' Samantha couldn't help stiffening.

'You don't have to look like that,' he said harshly. 'I didn't go to see her. She came to see me as soon as she heard I was back in town. She started fishing around for information about you as usual, and between one remark and another she gave herself away.' His mouth quirked with sardonic humour.

'Oh, how did she do that?' exclaimed Samantha, relaxing again.

'Well, I didn't tell her exactly what had happened to you,' he explained. 'I just said you hadn't been in the best of health. So she said you'd seemed perfectly well when she'd last seen you and I asked her, quite casually, when that had been.

You'd been windsurfing, she said, and went on to suggest that perhaps you'd overdone it and that's why you weren't well.' His grin widened. 'It was then I asked how could she have known you'd been windsurfing on the day you were taken ill when she had left the island.' His chuckle of laughter had a malicious sound. 'I'd never seen Morgana go red before. I pounced while she was disconcerted and accused her of having met you on the steps and pushing you off them.'

'What did she say?'

'She spluttered for a few seconds, said it was all an accident, that you'd tried to push her aside and she'd only been defending herself against your attack on her.'

'And then?'

'I told her to get out and never to come near me or you again. And that if she did bother us I'd have no hesitation in accusing her in public of trying to injure you. She left.'

Craig stood up and went out into the kitchen. He returned with his flask and poured more brandy into his glass, then sat down beside her again. He sipped the brandy, put the glass down and leaned back, turning his head to look at her.

'So now that we've got rid of Morgana, supposing you tell me what it was you were going to tell me before you met her on the steps,' he drawled softly.

Samantha looked away from his shrewd bright gaze and down at the brandy in her glass. Suddenly the blood was boiling in her veins and roaring in her ears, and she knew it wasn't the brandy that was having that effect on her. It was being close to Craig.

'How did you find out I'd left Antigua?' she asked, deliberately avoiding his question.

'Howard told me when I phoned Cliff House hoping to speak to you and to tell him I was flying out to see you again. He told me you'd come to London and asked me what I was going to do to stop you from divorcing me. Ever since he'd heard that you'd been to see a lawyer about a divorce he's been on about that. He's got some bee in his bonnet about you doing to me what my mother did to him. That's one of the reasons he invited you out to Antigua.'

'I know. He told me.'

'It's also why I chased after you through the islands; at least it's one of the reasons, and it's also why I asked you to pretend our separation was over.'

'To please Howard?' she queried.

'To shut him up and to stop him telling me how to run my life,' he retorted curtly. 'To stop him criticising you and saying you're like my mother.'

'And the other reasons?' she asked.

'One was to convince Morgana that she didn't have a hope in hell of busting up our marriage just so that she and I could get married once Conrad had taken over Clifton Enterprises.'

'Has he taken over Clifton's?'

'Yes. It's all done. He and I were able to persuade Dad to sell his shares to Taylor's Inc:'

'But what about you? What about your share of Clifton's?' she asked.

'I sold out before Dad did.'

'Why?'

'Because I was offered a good price and I wanted the money to put into my own business.'

'You have a business of your own?' she gasped.

'I have,' Craig assured her.

'You've never told me.'

'You never seemed particularly interested in what I did once I'd left the house in the morning to go to town,' he retorted dryly.

'Well, I suppose I . . . I just assumed you went to Clifton's,' she muttered defensively, and drank more brandy. 'What is your business?'

'Financing TV productions, syndicated news programmes, talk shows, that sort of thing—films for TV. For some time I've not only felt but I've known that the future lies in video rather than in newspaper and magazine publishing, because whether we like it or not we've brought up a generation of people that prefers to look and see more than they want to read. The business has grown and grown and is going to grow even bigger, so I wanted out of Clifton Enterprises to have more time to devote to its development.' Craig frowned. 'I was also hoping to have more time to spend with my wife,' he added stiffly.

There was silence. Samantha sipped more brandy and waited, sure that he had more to say. At last he went on slowly, not looking at her, his frown deepening,

'The most important reason for asking you to pretend our separation was over was the hope that it would become more than a pretence. I hoped that once we were together again we would stay together.' He sighed heavily. 'But I guess that was just wishful thinking on my part,' he added with a shrug, and looked at her suddenly, grey eyes flashing coldly to hers. 'When are you going to start divorce proceedings?' he asked curtly.

The question stung, like a dagger point pricking her skin. Brandy spilled on her skirt as her hand shook. Hastily she put the glass on the table.

'I . . . I'm not.'

'Did you say you're not?' he whispered, shifting closer to her, and the familiar fragrance of him wafted about her.

'Yes. I . . . I never intended to divorce you,' she replied, gripping her hands together on her knee because they wanted to reach out and touch his face, to stroke away the new lines she could see that had been carved into his tanned skin; not the lines of laughter about his eyes and mouth, they had been there before, but the lines created by cynical thoughts, by the exertion of self-control, possibly by suffering.

'Then why did you go to see that lawyer?' he demanded.

'I was going to ask him to write to you suggesting that we met to discuss a divorce,' she began to explain, and suddenly memories of how hurt and desperate she had been when he hadn't written to her or come to see her at the end of the two years surged through her and she blurted, 'Oh, I didn't know what to do! The two years were over and you'd been so silent and aloof all that time. I had to do something to . . . to jolt you somehow and remind you that I still existed and that we were still married, because you seemed to have forgotten!' Her voice rang out, shrill with bitterness.

'I hadn't forgotten. I did my best to forget, though, immersing myself in business, working hard, travelling . . .'

'Going about with Morgana,' she interrupted

him, jealousy of the time he had been apart from her twisting through her.

'No, never that,' he said forcibly.

'With other women, then. She told me you hadn't been faithful to me when I met her on the cliffside steps that day,' she hissed.

'She was making trouble as usual,' Craig retorted, his eyes beginning to glitter dangerously. 'And you as always believed her.'

'Do you deny then that there've been other women?' Samantha persisted, blinded by her jealousy to the danger signals.

'I dated a couple of women, yes, but there was nothing serious. They weren't important. I've been faithful to you in my fashion.' His lips twisted cynically. 'But you're not going to tell me you didn't go out with another man in all that time, because I know differently. I know about Lyndon Barry.'

'But I told you, I didn't make love with him or sleep with him.' Her lips were beginning to tremble. She wanted to throw herself against him and tell him she didn't want to argue with him any more, but she couldn't; something was still making her hold back.

'Neither did I want to,' he replied, the lines of cynicism deepening. 'But I have to admit I've not found it easy to practise celibacy.'

Samantha flinched away from that and sprang to her feet. Immediately Craig was on his feet too, watching her warily.

'Then there's nothing more to be said,' she muttered, turning away from him. 'Please go now and leave me alone.'

Behind her she heard his breath hiss as he drew it in savagely.

'No!' he retorted, and taking hold of her arm pulled sharply, swinging her round to face him. 'I'm not going and I'm not leaving you alone. I did that two years ago. I gave into your wishes. I left you here to do what you wanted to do. I went along with that idea of your mother's that you were too young to know your own mind when I asked you to marry me, that I rushed you into it . . .'

'To defy your father,' she retorted, interrupting him. 'You married me to defy your father because he wanted you to marry Morgana. He'd arranged it with Conrad Taylor. He told me.' She broke off, afraid suddenly of the expression in his eyes. He was glaring at her as if he wanted to hit her.

'I married you because I fell in love with you!' he shouted at her. 'And for no other reason. No matter what my father or your mother might have said about me.'

'You don't have to shout,' she whispered.

'But it seems that I do,' he replied, lowering his voice. 'You don't hear me unless I do. No, that isn't right,' he raked his hair with his fingers in a gesture of exasperation. 'You hear me, but don't believe me,' he added wearily. 'You prefer to believe what your mother has said about me rather than to trust me. You've believed Morgana more than you've believed me.' His lips curved in a sneer. 'You don't know what loving or being married involves. You think only of yourself.'

He turned away from her, picked up his glass from the table and tossed off the remains of the brandy and slammed it down on to the table again. Smitten to silence by his criticism of her, Samantha could only stand and stare at him, unaware of the stricken expression on her face.

Craig looked at her sadly for a few moments, then stepped towards her again.

'Listen—just listen to me for once. I fell in love for the first time in my life when I met you. But I didn't know I had until after I'd left London and gone back to Canada. When I did realise it I came right back as soon as I could and asked you to marry me,' he said softly. He took hold of both her arms as if by touching her he could convince her. Samantha was sure he didn't know how hard he was gripping her, but suddenly she didn't care, because he was saying at last what she had always wanted to hear and what she had once . . . how long ago that seemed now . . . believed to be true. He was telling her he had married her because he had fallen in love with her.

'Are you listening, Samantha?' he asked, gently and almost imperceptibly drawing her closer to him.

'Yes . . . yes, I'm listening. Oh, why haven't you told me this before?' she moaned.

'I guess because I thought you knew,' he replied slowly. 'I've never been one to talk a lot about my feelings. I much prefer to act, to do rather than to talk,' he added with a glimmer of a self-mocking smile. 'When I married you I obeyed the urgings of my heart. I did what I felt was instinctively right for me. And I believed you did the same.'

'I . . . I thought I did too,' she whispered.

'The first year of our marriage was great, or so I thought,' Craig continued. 'Then you began to change. You began to listen to what other people said about me instead of listening to your own heart. And . . . well, I had to let you go. I had to leave you here because you said it was what you wanted.' He let go of her arms and put his arms around her to hold her closely. 'But I'm not going to do that again. I'm not leaving you. You'll only run away if I do, like you ran away from Antigua when I left you there. I'm staying, and before tonight is through you're going to admit that you want our separation to be over as much as I do!'

He took hold of her hair and jerked her head back, and kissed her with such force that her lips felt burned. She had no defence. The dark urgent longing sprang up within her, and had to be satisfied. Her arms wound around his neck and her lips parted in passionate response.

'But why—why didn't you come before?' she whispered breathlessly when they were both sitting down again on the sofa with their arms still around each other. 'If you wanted to end the separation why didn't you come when the two years was over?'

'Because I was waiting to hear from you. I thought the first move should come from you. And it did.' Craig's grin was rueful. 'But not quite in the way I'd hoped. It came through my father. He told me about your visit to a lawyer. I was all set to fly here, to see you and to try to persuade you to come back to me, when he suggested a meeting in Antigua. We met, and my passionate pursuit of my runaway wife began. I hope it's ended here and now. Has it?'

He stroked her cheek with a gentle forefinger, all the time looking at her with eyes that were warm with desire.

'Yes,' Samantha whispered. 'I . . . I was going to tell you I wanted our separation to be over when . . . when I met Morgana on the steps. I was going

to tell you when I began to feel better, but . . . but
you'd gone away and I thought you didn't want
me any more.'

'I wanted you. I love you and I want you now,'
he said fiercely, passion making his voice throb.
His glance shifted from her eyes to her lips. His
head tipped towards her and his lips parted. 'Will
you have me to be your lover and your husband
again, Samantha?'

'Oh, yes, I will!' she replied, all the doubts and
suspicions that had tormented her wilting and
dying before his avowal of love, then she did what
she knew was instinctively right for her and for
him. She obeyed the urgings of her heart and
kissed him on the mouth, giving of herself
completely, without holding anything back.

A long time later, as they lay in the confines of
her single bed, where they had recently consum-
mated the end of their separation and the
resumption of their marriage, she asked,

'Where will we live?'

'Wherever you would like to live,' Craig
replied generously, stretching his legs against hers
in lazy contentment and trailing his fingertips over
the curve of her bare arm as if its silken
smoothness fascinated him.

'In the house near Toronto?' she asked, rubbing
her cheek against the rough hairiness of his chest and
shifting a hand from his waist to stroke his hip.

'No. We can't live there—I sold it.'

She lifted her head to peer at him in the faint
light that slanted in through the window from the
street lamp outside.

'You sold that lovely house?' she exclaimed.
'Why?'

'A, because you once said you hated it. B, because I couldn't bear to live in it once you had left it. C, because I received a great offer for it that I couldn't resist.'

'Oh, is that all you ever think about? Buying and selling and always to make a profit?' Samantha demanded indignantly.

'No, not always. Often I think of you and how much I like making love with you or just being with you. No, don't move away. I like you there, leaning over me, because I can do this and this.' His lips were warm and tantalising against the softness of her breasts. 'Aren't you glad I came here today?' he whispered.

'Yes,' she moaned as the most delightful sensations tingled through her.

'Love me?' he demanded breathlessly, and again his lips blazed a marauding trail across her skin and she moaned again in enjoying the exquisite torture.

'I love you. I love you very much,' she whispered.

'Then prove it,' he challenged thickly.

So she did, her mouth opening over his, her hands searching his body until, unable to resist her any longer, he probed the depths of her being again and satisfaction came in a sweet slow fusion expressive of their tenderest feelings for each other.

Next morning, as they breakfasted together in the flat, Craig suggested that they might spend a third of each year living in Antigua and cruising among the islands; another third in Canada and another third in England.

'But we'd need to be millionaires to do that!' Samantha gasped.

'We are millionaires,' he reminded her dryly. 'At least, I am, and when my father dies I stand to be even wealthier. How about this? Winter in the Caribbean, springtime in England, high summer and early fall in Canada? My mother once said it's the only way to get the most and the best out of those three areas, and I'm inclined to agree with her. And since it's almost spring here now we could start looking for a place to buy today. Would you like that?'

'Yes, I would. Oh, I do love you, Craig!'

'I suspect it's only a sort of cupboard love,' he teased her. 'You love me only when I do something that pleases you or when I let you have your own way.' Across the table he eyed her narrowly. 'Do you still want to continue with your career?' he asked cautiously.

'Oh, I forgot—I'm supposed to phone Marilyn Dowell,' she exclaimed, jumping to her feet and going through to the living room.

'Why?' he asked, following her.

'She phoned me on Friday and asked me if I'd like to go back to work at *Woman's Insight*,' she replied, and picked up the receiver Craig stepped over to her, his hand closing over hers.

'It isn't necessary for you to phone her,' he said.

'But I said I'd get back to her,' she retorted. 'Oh, I suppose you don't want me to take the job,' she accused as he forced her hand down, replacing the receiver on its rest.

'There isn't a job at *Woman's Insight* for you,' he said. 'Marilyn was just using the offer of a job as an excuse to call you at this address to find out if you were here.'

'Oh. Why would she do that?' she exclaimed.

'I asked her to,' he said. 'I called her from Toronto on Friday morning and asked her to find out if you were here. She called me back soon after she'd spoken to you and I was able to go ahead and make arrangements to fly here. I had to make sure you were really here before setting of in pursuit of you again, you know.' He frowned and gave her a thoughtful glance. 'Do you mind very much that there isn't a job at *Woman's Insight* for you? If you would like to go back there I'm sure I could arrange something, even though Clifton Enterprises no longer own it.'

She studied his face, wondering how sincere the offer was.

'You mean that?' she asked. 'You wouldn't object if I went back to work?'

'I wouldn't like it, but I wouldn't object,' he replied coolly. 'I've learned the hard way that you're entitled to live your own life the way you want to. You have to decide for yourself if you still want a career. Were you going to take the job?'

'I . . . I don't think so,' she confessed. 'I don't really know. In a way it's a relief not to have to decide whether to take it or not. You see, I was afraid Howard might have pressured Marilyn into offering it to me in the same way he'd pressured her into giving me the sack. I didn't want to be under an obligation to him. And now . . . I don't want to be under an obligation to you either. Not for a job. So the answer is no, I don't want you to try and arrange anything with *Woman's Insight*. I don't want you putting pressure on Marilyn Dowell on my account, using her to further your own ends.' She noticed a glint of mockery in his eyes, the slight ironic curl to his lips. 'Oh, you're just as bad as Howard,' she flared suddenly, 'checking on me, spying on me . . .'

'Pursuing you,' Craig put in softly, sliding his arms around her. '*Loving* you. I've only done what I've done because I love and care for you. I even left you alone for two years because I love you and could guess you needed time away from me, to see our marriage, our friendship, in a better perspective; because I knew I'd rushed you into marrying me. I had to rush you because I was afraid of never having you and never getting to know you any better.' He drew in his breath sharply. 'God, what more can I say to you to convince you that you matter to me more than anyone else in the world? Do you understand what I'm saying, my love, my one and my *only* love?'

'I'm trying,' she whispered, shaken to the core by this revelation of the depths and strength of his feelings for her, then she drew his head down so that she could kiss him, knowing in her heart that she would never run away from such love again.

Harlequin® Plus

A WORD ABOUT THE AUTHOR

Ever since she can remember, Flora Kidd has cherished a longing to sail the seas — not on a big ocean liner, but in a sailboat. This great love brought her into contact with her husband-to-be, Wilf, who shared her dream. And over the years, they and their four children have sailed the waters of the Old World and the New (today they make their home in New Brunswick, one of Canada's maritime provinces).

Flora's decision to write came about while she was living in a seaside village in the south of Scotland. Looking for something to read, she borrowed several romance novels and afterward remarked to a friend, "I think I could write a story like these." To which the friend replied, "Maybe you could, but would anyone want to read it?"

That was the necessary challenge! Flora's first Romance, *Nurse at Rowanbank* (#1058), was published in 1966 and her first Presents, *Dangerous Pretence* (#212), appeared in 1977. She is now a best-selling author of more than twenty Romances and fifteen Presents.

THE GOLDEN CAGE

The first Harlequin American Romance Premier Edition
by bestselling author ANDREA DAVIDSON

Harlequin American Romance Premier Editions is an exciting new program of longer–384 pages!–romances. By our most popular Harlequin American Romance authors, these contemporary love stories have superb plots and true-to-life characters–trademarks of Harlequin American Romance.

The Golden Cage, set in modern-day Chicago, is the exciting and passionate romance about the very real dilemma of true love versus materialism, a beautifully written story that vividly portrays the contrast between the life-styles of the run-down West Side and the elegant North Shore.

Watch for *The Golden Cage* at your favorite bookstore in April, or send your name, address and zip or postal code, along with a check or money order for $3.70 (includes 75¢ for postage and handling) payable to Harlequin Reader Service, to: Harlequin Reader Service

In the U.S.
Box 52040
Phoenix, AZ 85072-2040

In Canada
649 Ontario Street
Stratford, Ontario N5A 6W2

GC-2